P9-BYN-972

Blast from the past

Aaron was over between two glowing screens. His hands were splaying out over the keyboards. He entered five or six digits. Then it happened. Both screens lit up like Las Vegas. Full-color supergraphics surged. I smelled everything—smoke, flowers, furniture polish. I blinked.

When I looked again, Aaron was still there. But somebody else was in the room, standing between us. One second she wasn't there. The next she was.

"Amiable characters, fleet pacing and witty, in-the-know narration will keep even the non-bookish interested."

—*Publishers Weekly*

BOOKS BY RICHARD PECK

Are You in the House Alone?

Father Figure

The Ghost Belonged to Me

Ghosts I Have Been

The Great Interactive Dream Machine

Lost in Cyberspace

Representing Super Doll

Through a Brief Darkness

LOST IN CYBERSPACE

LOST IN CYBERSPACE

Richard Peck

PUFFIN BOOKS

PUFFIN BOOKS
Published by the Penguin Group
Penguin Putnam Inc., 375 Hudson Street, New York, New York 10014, U.S.A.
Penguin Books Ltd, 27 Wrights Lane, London W8 5TZ, England
Penguin Books Australia Ltd, Ringwood, Victoria, Australia
Penguin Books Canada Ltd, 10 Alcorn Avenue, Toronto, Ontario, Canada M4V 3B2
Penguin Books (N.Z.) Ltd, 182-190 Wairau Road, Auckland 10, New Zealand

Penguin Books Ltd, Registered Offices: Harmondsworth, Middlesex, England

First published in the United States of America by Dial Books for Young Readers,
a division of Penguin Books USA Inc., 1995
Published in Puffin Books, 1997

7 9 10 8

Copyright © Richard Peck, 1995
All rights reserved

THE LIBRARY OF CONGRESS HAS CATALOGED THE DIAL EDITION AS FOLLOWS:
Peck, Richard.
Lost in cyberspace / by Richard Peck. p. cm.
Summary: While dealing with changes at home, sixth-grader Josh and his friend Aaron use the computers at their New York City prep school to travel through time, learning some secrets from the school's past and improving Josh's home situation.
ISBN 0-8037-1931-0
[1. Time travel—Fiction. 2. Schools—Fiction. 3. Brothers and sisters—Fiction.]
I. Title.
PZ7.P338Lo 1995 [Fic]—dc20 94-48330 CIP AC

Puffin Books ISBN 0-14-037856-1

Printed in the United States of America

Except in the United States of America, this book is sold subject to the condition that it shall not, by way of trade or otherwise, be lent, re-sold, hired out, or otherwise circulated without the publisher's prior consent in any form of binding or cover other than that in which it is published and without a similar condition including this condition being imposed on the subsequent purchaser.

This book is dedicated
with thanks
to Jana Fine and Pat Scales

1

The Mesozoic Era

After the separation, Dad moved to Chicago, and Mom decided to go back to work, so she was practicing getting up early. She'd bought some new outfits. Heather and I were dressed for school. I go to the Huckley School for Boys, so I was in dress code:

black blazer
blue-and-white Huckley tie
big shirt
gray flannel pants
any shoes but sneakers

Heather goes to the Pence School for Girls:

white blouse, choice of style, with collar
Pence plaid skirt
any shoes but sneakers

Heather's shoe statement was lace-up black blobs with stainless steel eyelets and tire-tread soles. Each of her shoes weighed an easy six pounds.

"There are children with tragic foot deformities who have to wear corrective shoes much better looking than those," Mom often said to Heather. "And cheaper."

This morning Mom had some news for us. It was about somebody named Fenella, who was coming from England to live with us. Mom had found Fenella on an Internet link-up called "Au Pair Exchange."

"And what's an O Pear supposed to be?" Heather was tearing open a Pop-Tart and examining its insides, which is a thing she does. "It sounds like a baby-sitter who never leaves. Who needs her? I'm virtually thirteen and emotionally fourteen. I missed the Gifted and Talented Program by *this much*. I can sit myself. I'll O Pear Josh."

She jerked a thumb at me. And I'm only one grade behind her. "I'll be the O Pear who never leaves," Heather said.

I slid out of my chair and checked out the window for the school bus. We live twelve floors above Fifth Avenue. The trees over in Central Park were bare branches with wrinkled balloons left over from summer. The Huckley bus was held up at the light on the corner. It's a Chrysler minivan with a blue-and-white paint job. Heather's Pence bus was in the distance behind a tie-up.

"Buses," I said.

"Don't think of Fenella as a baby-sitter," Mom said.

"I'm not thinking about her at all," Heather said. "She's the farthest thing from my mind. And where are we going to put her? We use the maid's room for storage."

"And don't think of her as a maid," Mom said. "Au pairs are not baby-sitters. And they aren't servants. They're English girls from very nice backgrounds. They come over here to help out with families and to see American life. They're here to expand their horizons, and ours."

Heather said, "My horizons are already—"

But Mom said, "Whoa," because I was heading for the door. She had new glasses with giant lenses for her upcoming career. She looked me over. Standing, I'm as tall as she is sitting. "How did you learn to tie a tie that well?" She peered at me. "It even has a little dimple under the knot. That's professional work."

"Practice," I said.

"Is the day coming when you won't need your old ma for anything?"

"Not right away," I said.

"I have the final interview today," Mom said, "at Barnes Ogleby."

"B.O.," Heather said.

"I'll be home before you two are unless they let school out early again. Why can't schools run the full day anymore?"

"Because we're pressured enough." Heather clutched her forehead. "We need a lot more time off than we get."

"All the more reason for Fenella. I don't want you turning into a couple of latchkey kids," Mom said. "Wet or dry?" she said to me.

"Dry as possible."

She planted a careful kiss on my cheek. It was hardly damp, and she didn't have her lipgloss on yet.

I didn't give Fenella any more thought. I mainly think about what's happening now. When I left the apartment for school, Heather was still popping her tart. We try not to take the same elevator.

Aaron Zimmer was on it, coming down from the penthouse. He's in my year at Huckley, but shorter. We call him the A-to-Z man because of his name and because he knows everything from A to Z. Some of what he knows is actual fact. Some of it is just stuff he says.

"Yo," we said. I stick my homework into whatever book. Everybody but Aaron carries gear to school in a backpack. He carries a briefcase-style laptop computer with a certain amount of software. Even without storing it electronically, he has a lot of signal compression in his biological memory bank. He's what they used to call a smart kid.

"Six hundred and sixty-five more class periods till summer," he said. "I estimate that at seven classes a day, five days a week, allowing for holidays, spring break, and field trips."

"What about—"

"I've factored in fire drills. The field trip today is dinosaurs."

The Huckley School catalogue tells parents that all its students are to be interactively computer literate for the challenges of twenty-first century corporate competition.

This means they've walled off one end of the media center and have a couple of terminals in there. I'm not that much into it. Also, I spell better in real life than on the keyboard. Aaron has named the computer room the Black Hole. That's his personal name for it, possibly because it doesn't have natural light. He's in there most of the day. You can sign out of classes and go there if you can get a teacher to cover for you.

They tell us that in the future we won't have to leave our screens for global video-conferencing across the information superhighway. All we'll need is a mouse and a modem and we'll never need to go outdoors.

But we get out quite a bit for field trips. So we were looking at another day at the Natural History Museum. You can get all this edutainment on CD-ROM. But in the winter we have two field trips a week to keep the restlessness down.

At the museum, they threw our class in with the fourth and fifth grades. The fourth graders aren't even in middle school yet, but we integrate with them for field trips to get them ready for us. Even the fourth graders have been coming to see the dinosaurs for years.

"All they do is stand around like dorks," said a fifth grader, meaning the dinosaurs. "What this place needs is some electronic manipulation. They could use some digital film techniques."

"Kids," Aaron said, shaking his head.

We passed up the headphones. Aaron had the whole dinosaur evolution stored and was happy to display his own personal version of it.

"The jury is still hung about whether dinosaurs were hot-blooded or cold like your contemporary reptiles," he remarked. "The speed of their movements argues for hot blood."

We moved into the Hall of Mongolian Vertebrates.

"In Asian deserts fossilized nestlings have been uncovered along with clutches of eggs. This means dinosaurs conducted family life. To defend against the meat-eaters, the larger herbivores developed a herd mentality."

A herd of fourth graders were hanging around us by now. Aaron talked them right through to the extinction of dinosaurs, touching lightly on the giant asteroid theory.

They listened, but some of them were still confused by "fossilized nestlings."

"Say hello to the baluchitheres," he said in passing, "ancient cousins of your modern rhino."

Then he summed up by saying, "The only certain fact about dinosaurs is that no species was ever purple and named Barney."

The fourth graders stared.

Now the museum cafeteria was in sight. A huge, long-necked, small-headed shadow fell over us.

It was Mr. Headbloom, the teacher in charge. He has us for homeroom, and he's our reading teacher. He calls the reading class Linear Decoding. You'd think teachers would be impressed by Aaron. He has all this knowledge he doesn't even have to call up on a screen. But with teachers he's not that popular. Mr. Headbloom is glad to sign him out of class to go to the Black Hole anytime Aaron wants.

"Zimmer," Mr. Headbloom said, "knock off the voice-over and let the fourth graders interface with the exhibits as units."

As the old Huckley teachers like Mr. L. T. Thaw die off, they're replaced by mouse potatoes like Mr. Headbloom who talk like this. We went in and did lunch.

2

The Ultimate Computer

Aaron had goat cheese on seven-grain bread, being a vegetarian—herbivore. I had the beef burrito.

"I don't know," I said. "Dinosaurs just don't do it for me anymore. I mean, they're all dead and gone, right? Who'd want them around anyway? Hitting a deer on the highway is bad enough."

Aaron had his laptop on the lunch table. He was idly punching up something on it with his left hand, then squinting at his screen.

"Look, the past is over," I said. "It's okay for museums, but we've got enough problems without digging up the old days. Am I right or what?"

Aaron dug a grain out from between his teeth. "I have a theory." He has a lot of them. "And I think modern cybernetics will bear me out sooner or later. As we know, science is slow."

His left hand was still playing his laptop like a piano. He can think out of at least two compartments of his brain at the same time.

"As I see it, there are a couple of ways to approach the past. You can dig it up, like dinosaurs, which is basically pre-electronic."

"There's cloning too," I said. "DNA and like that."

"Forget cloning. That's not experiencing the past. That's reproducing it."

"There's virtual reality," I said.

"That's show business," Aaron said.

"Or you can get into your time machine," which was my last idea.

Aaron sighed. "Josh, I can read your mind. Time machine to you means this thing made out of sheet metal with ten-speed gears, flashing lights, and little puffs of smoke coming out of a tailpipe. A contraption."

"With seat belts," I said.

"Forget it," he said. "Grow up." Sometimes he can look at you just like a teacher.

"You can dig up the past. Or you can really test the electronic limits and actually be there. It's a question of dialing into the cosmic internet. The past isn't necessarily over. It's just piping in on a parallel plane." Aaron ran a finger around his collar, which is a thing he does. I think his mom still ties his tie. "Do you follow me?"

"Sure," I said.

"No, you don't. You're like this in class. You're breathing steady. Your eyes are open. But nobody's home. Your modem's unplugged. Let me try it another way." He tapped the table with a finger covered in goat-cheese crumbs.

"We're looking ahead to maybe five hundred TV channels available to the general viewing public."

"So?"

"So how about five hundred and one?"

"You mean the five hundred and first channel is the real past if you could just find a way of calling it up?"

"You're scanning in the right direction," Aaron said, "but I know how you think. You picture yourself sitting in front of a screen viewing the past like an old movie, with a bottle of Snapple in your hand."

"But big screen," I said, "and better than VHS quality."

Aaron rolled his eyes, so I said, "What you're saying is that the past is still happening if you know where to look?"

"Cyberspatially," said the A-to-Z man. "Or in layman's terms, yes."

"Just how many people are going to be able to channel-surf into another time?" I try not to swallow all Aaron's theories. I try to be skeptical.

He shrugged. "Who can say? Maybe we're already doing it and don't notice. We sleep a third of the time. Teenagers sleep more than that. Who knows where you are when you're asleep? Not all your circuitry is shut down. Think about dreams."

"I dream a lot about falling."

"Who doesn't? That's the first fear babies have. We haven't been babies for ten years. Dreams are strange, and the whole world's strange to a baby, right? And scary. Maybe dreams aren't memories. Maybe they're happening."

"Then you wake up and you're back to real time?" I said.

"Both times are real," Aaron said. "The forward-movement idea of time is a pretech human way of explaining the unknown. It's a primitive invention, like the rotary-dial phone."

"And I have this dream where we're taking a test at school, except it isn't exactly Huckley. And if I fail this test, I'm in deep—"

"Perfect example," Aaron said. "That could be something from a hundred years ago when flunking a test was serious. You could be living the experience of a kid in a really strict school, in England or somewhere. I mean it's not about now, right? Buster Brewster has flunked every test since preschool. And does Huckley throw him out or keep him back a year or beat him with paddles? No such luck. Not as long as his parents keep paying tuition."

Aaron shouldn't even have mentioned Buster Brewster, because Buster himself appeared at our table. We don't have bullies at Huckley. We call them hyperactive. Buster was the main one in our grade.

He whacked the back of Aaron's head and reached across him for our salt shaker. Buster was going from table to table, loosening the tops of the salt shakers like he does in the school cafeteria. There's nothing too original about his thinking. He wrenched ours loose with his mighty fist. Salt rained all over the table.

"Don't even think about tightening that," he said.

Buster's voice hasn't changed yet, but it's lower than ours. "Make my day, wusses." Then he lumbered on to the next table.

"Be nice if Buster Brewster entered another time frame and forgot to come back," I said, but quietly. "Seriously, though, do you think it's possible to make contact with other times, outside of dreams?"

"Josh," Aaron said, making shapes in the salt, "we've already got video beamed over phone wire. We've got phone calls digitized over TV cable. We've got data-based interactivity going in every direction. We're talking information explosion. We're talking new windows of opportunity. Or in layman's terms, anything's possible."

I'd polished off my burrito. Aaron was picking up scattered grains on his plastic plate with a wet, salty finger. Somehow this annoyed me.

"Like you're fine-tuning yourself, right?" I said to him. "Like you could be time-warped into another age, right?"

"I'm in early stages with it," Aaron said. "And remember, generally speaking, technology is way behind concept.

"And remember this too, Josh." He stared across the table at me like a red-headed owl. "Artificial intelligence is the buzzword of the age and the wave of the future. But the human brain is the ultimate computer."

All this talk about time and distance reminded me of Fenella for some reason.

"We're getting an O Pear."

Aaron pushed back his tray and ran a hand through his hair. Being carrot-red, it suits a vegetarian.

"Tell me about it, Josh." Sometimes he sounds like a guidance counselor.

I hadn't meant to tell him a thing. I hadn't even mentioned that my mom and dad were separated. Dad had only been gone three months and a week, and usually called Sunday nights. I hadn't gotten around to mentioning it to anybody. I didn't even like mentioning it to myself.

"Your mom's getting some help around the house now your dad's left and she's going back to work at Barnes Ogleby?"

I stared. "Aaron, how do you know my dad's—not around? How do you have access to all this personal data about my family?"

"Vince. The doorman. Day shift. Doormen know it all. Who's there. Who's not. What we eat, because they see the grocery deliveries. Your mom's not having the groceries delivered anymore. She's cutting down expenses by carrying them home. Doormen read our mail."

"They read our mail?"

"The envelopes. How else could they sort them? Your dad's writing from a 60611 zip code. Chicago, right? You people ought to get E-mail."

"It's just a trial separation," I said, though I wasn't too sure about that. Maybe I should ask Vince.

"Is it a French au pair or a German one?" Aaron asked. "Because they'll try to teach you the language.

Bonjour, mes enfants; Guten Tag, Kinder—that kind of thing."

"English," I said, "but our apartment is filling up with women."

I didn't have to say I wanted Dad back. Aaron could figure that out. His dad and mom are together. But his mom is his dad's third wife, so you never know.

The field trip shot the day. We only went back to Huckley to catch our buses home. Mom was already there when I came in.

"I got the job," she said. She was in jeans and a sweatshirt, clearing everything out of Dad's old den. He hadn't taken much but his computer and fax. I thought that was a good sign. But now Mom was sweeping clean. She was dusting Dad's empty shelves.

"What a long face," she said, fingering my chin. "It's just for now, Josh. Really. I'm tidying things away so we can put Fenella in here. We've always used it as a guest room anyway. Think of Fenella as a—helpful guest. She'll be good for Heather. Heather needs a . . . role model."

So Fenella was nearer than I knew.

I dreamed that night, big-time and nonstop. It was about Aaron and me at the Natural History Museum. It was us, but it wasn't exactly the museum. It was actual Mesozoic times. We weren't wearing anything except blue-and-white Huckley ties, which is typical of my dreams. As we trudged along through the swamp, mud and twigs seeped between our toes.

"Primeval ooze," the dream Aaron said.

Volcanoes were erupting in the distance. Some really scary things were flying around on webbed wings. All my dreams are colorized. Aaron was eating a carrot. When he clutched my dream arm, we took cover under a plant with giant leaves.

A huge, long-necked, small-headed shadow fell over us. It blotted out the sky. Aaron and I grabbed each other. The leaf we were hiding under turned transparent. And this dinosaur spotted us. Its head wasn't so small anymore. A snaky neck coiled, and it was coming down at us, and it was all teeth.

"Tyrannosaurus Regina," Aaron whispered. "Cretaceous period. Meat-eater."

Now its eyes were zeroing in on me. And its face was changing. Now it was half-human with big brown eyes.

"My name is Fenella," it said. "Think of me as a helpful guest." Then its jaws opened wide.

That was enough to knock me out of bed. I fought my way up toward being awake. It's a long way from the Mesozoic Era. But I was nearly there. I could feel the sheet twisted under me. And I had on my pajamas, which is more than I was wearing in the dream.

I wasn't alone, though. Somehow Heather had horned in on my dream. But I was moving faster than she was. Her shoes were slowing her down.

3

The Club Scene

"Let's put our best feet forward," Mom said. She'd rounded up Heather and me to meet Fenella at the airport. She even hinted we might wear our school clothes.

"No way," Heather said. "We're only inmates during the day." She wanted to stay home because she said Camilla Van Allen might call. Heather says Camilla Van Allen is her best friend. But we hadn't seen anything of her.

"She'll leave a message for you on the machine," Mom told Heather. "If she calls."

Heather looked sulky in her parachute silk puffy jacket, jeans, and her biggest shoes. I wore the Bulls warm-up jacket Dad sent me from Chicago after one of the Sunday nights when he didn't call. We cabbed out to JFK Airport in the middle of the evening rush. Then

Fenella's flight was two hours late because snow was blowing. Only one runway was open.

That gave Mom time to run over the Au Pair Exchange printout. Fenella was seventeen, a recent "school leaver," whose interests included

reading
field hockey
gardening
needlework
flower-arranging
and gourmet cooking

Her career aspirations were in the areas of

teaching
editing children's books
or interior design

Halfway through the printout Heather wandered off to browse the airport arcade shops.

There was a fuzzy Xerox picture of Fenella in a school uniform and straw hat. It didn't look too recent and could have been anybody.

The contract said Fenella could be expected to "assist with light household work, food preparation, and child care, no more than twenty hours a week, with opportunities for extended travel experience in the United States." She had a right to her own room.

"Do we pay her, or does she pay us?"

"We pay her," Mom said.

Heather came back and said, "Let's eat." We went to

the Skyteria until they announced that the London plane was on the ground.

Passengers came pouring out through the Customs doors, pushing their luggage on carts. Mom kept the picture handy and was watching everybody. "Let's be very careful about our speech patterns," she said. "English people speak so beautifully."

I lost count after a hundred and eighty people. Aaron would have had his calculator with him. "Maybe she's not coming," Heather said, perking up. The waiting crowd was pretty much just us by now. Most of the people coming out were flight attendants. "When we see the pilot," Heather said, "let's leave."

Then the door banged open, and this girl appeared, dragging a giant laundry bag with tags. She was fairly giant herself, dressed in total, recycled black. Several layers over a black body stocking and big elf boots below.

But what you really noticed was her face. It was a large pale moon with black lips, three nose rings, and a small spider tattooed on her right cheekbone. The hat on top was hard to miss too. It had a big floppy brim pinned back by a bunch of black plastic flowers.

Heather blinked. "Beyond grunge," she said.

Mom was still looking for somebody to match the picture. But the girl came toward us, getting bigger and bigger. We weren't hard to spot. We were the only people left.

"Fenella here," she said, gazing over our heads with big sleepy brown eyes.

"Oh," Mom said. "Oh. I'm . . . Mrs. Lewis."

"I'm Josh," I said, staggering back because Fenella had dropped her laundry bag on me.

"I'm like amazed," Heather said, staring.

The snow was blowing out to sea, and the air was crisp and clear. You get a great look at Manhattan on a night like that: all the twinkling towers and the chains of lights on the bridges. Mom wanted to show Fenella the view. But she slept through it. She was zonked right to our door. We had to wake her up to get out of the cab.

"Jet lag," Mom said in a hushed voice. "It's just temporary. But I wonder if that spider is permanent."

Then Fenella dozed off in the elevator, slumped against the wall with her hat tipped down to her nose rings. She snored.

She slept for nineteen hours. By then it was Saturday evening. Mom was getting nervous. For one thing, she was going out that night. Behind a door, I heard her and Heather.

"It's not a date," Mom was saying. "Stop calling it a date. It's dinner and the theater with Mr. Ogleby, Jr. It's business. He's head of the accounting department, and he's welcoming me into the firm. He's just showing me professional courtesy. Should I wear my drop earrings, or are they too much?"

"It's a date," Heather said when she caught me listening outside the door. "Mom's dating again. We better get Fenella on her feet or Mom won't leave. She'll cancel Mr. Ogleby, Jr., and stay home with us. She'll want to pop popcorn and rerun *Honey, I Shrunk the Kids.*"

We cracked the door of Dad's den. The sofa folds out into a bed. There was a large lump in the middle of it. Fenella's hat was on Dad's desk, covering most of it.

"Hey, Fenella," Heather said. The lump moved. "It's like a whole different day. In fact, it's night again. Get up."

Fenella seemed to be on her hands and knees now, shaking her head. "Crikey," she said, or something like that.

Mom was dressed in her best and beginning to pace when Fenella came into the living room. She filled up the whole door. She'd taken off some of her black layers and left on the rest. We hadn't caught a good look at her with her hat off before. Hair sprang up like a stiff mop all around her head, and it was between maroon and purple. On her right cheekbone was a small human skull with a dagger through its eye socket. So the spider wasn't permanent.

"Oh," Mom said. "Feeling rested?"

"Feelin' like I just been jumped by a bunch of skinheads," Fenella said. "Feelin' like I was just kicked in the—"

The buzzer rang, and it was Mr. Ogleby, Jr. Mom had to go. "Maybe I should call when we get to the theater," she said at the door. She didn't feel any too good about leaving us.

"It's cool, Mom," Heather said. "We'll O Pear Fenella. She'll be fine." Then Heather gave me a look which she usually doesn't do.

After that we showed Fenella the kitchen. She stood in front of the refrigerator, making a few selections.

"Do you want to do some gourmet cooking?" Heather inquired, testing her.

"Some wot?" Fenella said. "You got Big Macs in this country yet?"

It wouldn't have surprised me if Fenella had wanted to call it a day and go back to bed. She didn't move fast even in her thinking. And I'll tell you this. She never did figure out what our names were. We followed as she roamed around the apartment, ending up at the living room windows. "Oy," she said or something like that. "It's night."

"I tried to tell you," Heather said.

"So let's go," Fenella said, beginning to stir.

Heather blinked. We're talking New York here, so we don't go out at night a lot. On the other hand, Heather began to see some possibilities. Anyway, maybe Fenella would be protection enough.

"Like where?" Heather said carefully.

"Like outta here is flippin' where," Fenella said. "Clubs and such."

"Clubs?" Heather had heard of them, but didn't know where they were.

"Clubs, raves, venues," Fenella said. She was waking up now. "I got some addresses. Downtown."

To us, downtown is anywhere south of Saks, and we don't go there. A strange, eager look came over Heather's face. "I don't think Josh can get in," she said, still carefully. "Of course, we could leave him at home."

"*You* couldn't get in like that." Fenella looked down

at Heather in her peach cableknit cardigan and then at me in my Bulls warm-up jacket, which I'm always wearing when I'm not wearing something else.

"You, Tiny Tim," Fenella said to me. "You got a school uniform? Coat and tie, something like that?" I nodded. "Go put it on. They'll think you're a midget." This could have been Fenella's little joke. But I didn't want to get left behind, so I went to change. Fenella pointed Heather to her room and followed her in.

In fifteen minutes the three of us were out in the hall, waiting for the elevator. I was in blazer and Huckley tie.

Fenella didn't look too different. She had her hat on, a major statement. She'd freshened the black on her lips and added a ring or two to her nose. From her laundry bag she'd come up with a long black cape. She looked like a cross between a vampire and a graduating senior.

Underneath, she had on a really micro-skirt, also black, with fishnet stockings. The stockings had holes in them with a lot of Fenella showing through.

But Heather was the center of attention, which she likes. Fenella had done her over. In fact, Heather had on Fenella's face. Her lips were coal-black. Fenella had even drawn in nose rings with her eyebrow pencil, along with a small coiled rattlesnake with fangs on Heather's cheek. Heather's hair is pale and preppy. But Fenella had wrapped it in a black scarf, turban-style. Heather's skirt was amazing. It wasn't any wider than a scarf itself. In this light it looked like shiny black leather.

"It's a plastic garbage bag folded and pinned behind," Heather whispered. "Fenella's a genius."

Heather wore her own panty hose, which she'd torn some serious holes in. She already had the right shoes. She looked like Minnie Mouse from Long Island, but older, which thrilled her.

The elevator door opened, and a man and woman were inside. The woman saw us and screamed. The man jammed a button, and the door closed in our faces. We took the next elevator. But the man and woman had been the Zimmers, Aaron's parents.

"Wot come over them?" Fenella wondered. Then we were past the doorman and out on Fifth Avenue. "Which way's downtown?" she asked, and we pointed her south. With her cape billowing behind her, Fenella was like a large pirate ship under full sail. There was a lot of space in that cape. I began to see how all three of us might get into a club.

"It's south of SoHo," said Fenella, who was a little better organized than she seemed. "Do we hoof it or wot?"

I had money, but didn't know what a cab that far downtown would cost. So I aimed us left on 68th Street for the subway entrance.

We rocketed downtown on a train. And I have to say there were some stranger sights on it than Heather and Fenella. Heather kept giving me looks with her new eyes, which had giant lashes painted in. She was pretty excited. We don't do the subway and certainly not after dark.

We got off way downtown in the warehouse district. But Fenella had a good sense of direction when it came to finding clubs. Finally we were walking along a dark street that was all stripped cars and fire escapes with icicles.

Then we were walking past a line of people who seemed to be looking for a Halloween party. Half of them were on Rollerblades. You had punk and post-punk. You had important hair and totally shaved. You had prom dresses with leg warmers. You had more tattoos than a tractor pull. You had everything from biker boots to bikinis. You had stuff you can't believe. At the front of the line two big guys were guarding a metal door.

"Right, you two," Fenella muttered to us, "under the cape and put a sock in it."

"Put a sock in what?" Heather asked.

"Shut your gob," Fenella explained. "Keep quiet."

Suddenly I was sandwiched between Heather and the back part of Fenella under the cape. The world got even darker.

Fenella had planned to talk us straight into the club, no waiting. But the big guys at the door were giving her static.

"Aw right, aw right," she said. "Don't get your knickers in a twist. I come all the flippin' way from Lunnun to get in this club. I get in all the Lunnun clubs. I'm a personal mate of Boy George. Wotcher mean, I'm too dressed down? 'Ere, stand aside, you miserable gits, or I'll have your guts for garters."

When she stamped her big elf boot, she nearly flattened one of my toes. My foot jerked back and caught Heather on the shin: one more hole for her panty hose.

"A right pair of yobbos you lot are," Fenella was telling the door guards. The cape flapped, and I realized she was putting up her fists.

She was about to punch out two bodybuilders of gorilla size. By now Heather had both hands around my neck, holding on. We'd never have gotten in that club anyway, not with all those extra legs under the cape.

Fenella was starting up the steps anyhow, fighting her way in. I tripped, but followed. Then the world shifted. Robo-hands slipped under Fenella's armpits. She was suddenly off the ground. Her big legs windmilled in every direction. Then we all seemed to be airborne and peeling out of the cape.

We hit frozen litter in the gutter between two stripped cars. A cheer went up from the waiting line of Halloweeners.

The next thing I remember is limping down a side street, listening to what Fenella was calling the two bouncers. They were probably pretty bad words in England. "Prats" was one of them, and "wallies" was another. Heather was beginning to trail behind because of her shoes.

No cab would pick us up, so we had to take the subway again.

Since we hadn't been out that long, I thought we might be home free. But Mom opened the door. She'd called from the theater, and her own voice answered her on the machine. She panicked and came home.

Now she was looking at us. Fenella's hat was still knocked sideways, with the skull on her cheek showing.

Her cape was crusty with gutter slush. Heather's turban was unwinding. But her drawn-on nose rings were hanging tough, and you could practically hear her snake rattle. She'd lost the pin, so she was holding what looked a lot like a narrow garbage bag around her waist. And she wouldn't get another wearing out of those panty hose. We looked like we'd been in a wreck, but not serious enough to feel sorry for. I was wearing school dress code, which made me look responsible, though I wasn't.

4

The Last of Fenella

We took Fenella out to JFK for her flight back to London the next day.

"As a single parent, I see I'm going to have to make a lot of split-second decisions," Mom said. "Fenella goes."

Frankly, Fenella didn't seem that surprised. This may have happened to her before in other countries.

Coming back into the city, I wanted to sit up front with the cabby. He didn't speak English. I thought that might be better than what Mom had to say. But they don't let you sit up front. You could be armed.

Mom sighed. "Fenella had no more judgment than you two." I was on one side of her, and Heather was on the other, staring out the window and trying not to be involved.

We'd been over everything last night. Now we had to go over it again. "All right, Josh," Mom said. "Who should be out at night in New York?"

"Adults," I mumbled, "in cars or cabs. Aboveground."

"And where should they be?"

"Well-lighted neighborhoods. Uptown, East Side preferably, except in the immediate Lincoln Center area."

But Mom couldn't let it go. "Planet Hollywood, I could understand," she said. "The Hard Rock Cafe maybe. Even the Harley-Davidson Cafe in a pinch."

"You could look at it as kind of a field trip," I said.

"Field trip, my foot," Mom said. "The only reason Fenella came over here is to go to so-called clubs in Tribeca and other battle zones that sell drugs to New Jersey teenagers."

Heather sighed. She was waiting for Mom to say "disco," which is a word out of Mom's past she uses sometimes.

"You could see at a glance Fenella was a night person," Mom said. "All she wanted to do was go to discos."

Heather looked around her at me.

"And don't think she wanted the two of you along. She only took you because it was her first night. Later, she'd have dumped you. I wouldn't know who was in charge of you or where you were."

"Mo-om, you don't need to know where I am all the time," Heather whined. "I'm virtually thirteen and emotionally—"

"If you were half as mature as you think you are," Mom said, "you wouldn't have walked past the doorman last night, twice, wearing nothing but a rag on your head, a snake on your face, and a Hefty bag."

"The Zimmers saw us too," I mentioned.

Mom slumped. "You don't mean to tell me that the Zimmers saw you."

"Put a sock in it, Josh," Heather said.

5

Muggers to the Fourth Power

The first field trip that next week was to the Museum of the City of New York. This is probably the most low-tech museum in town. But it's worth a trip, though probably not twice a semester. They had us in with the fourth and fifth grades again.

Most of what they've got in this museum is either under glass or roped off. But you have to watch the fourth and fifth graders. You've got to watch Buster Brewster like a hawk. Three teachers had to pry him loose from a scale model of the Empire State Building. Buster was being King Kong.

After that we had to walk with a teacher according to grade. Mr. Headbloom ran us through the history of the city: dioramas and room settings like "A Dutch Kitchen in Old Nieuw Amsterdam."

Somewhere after "Washington Inaugurated in Wall Street," I missed Aaron. He hadn't been giving his own voice-over because we were too close to Mr. Headbloom. One minute Aaron was there. The next he wasn't. I may have seen him darting up to the second floor. I may not have. Then we were gridlocked behind fourth graders who were hung up at "The Evolution of Hook and Ladder Companies."

Upstairs they've got complete rooms from historic houses. We were coming up on John D. Rockefeller's bedroom (1880). He was a rich tycoon who gave away dimes to show he was generous.

Heavy curtains, gas fixtures, many rugs, and a big bed, all in dim, old-fashioned light. The younger kids moved past the doorway at their top speed. We would have too, except Mr. Headbloom glanced into the bedroom and stopped cold. Sixth graders walked up his heels.

Mr. Rockefeller was in his bed. He died in 1937 at the age of ninety-eight. It says so on a plaque out in the hall. But there was a lump in his bed. I thought of Fenella, but it wasn't that large. What size Rockefeller was, I didn't know. By now he probably wouldn't be too big. The covers were pulled up. But the pillow was dented like there might be a head up there.

Mr. Headbloom looked around for Buster. But for once, he was with the rest of us. The lump in the bed moved. You had to be watching, but it did. "Is this real or multimedia?" somebody said.

Mr. Headbloom scanned up and down the hall,

checking for a museum guard. Then he took a quick, giant scissor-step over the rope across the door. "You," he said to Buster, who was about to go with him, "back."

We watched Mr. Headbloom tiptoe across the oriental carpets. It was cool because this was almost breaking and entering. How often do you see a teacher do that?

He got closer and closer to the bed. He reached down and pulled back the covers. Another rule broken.

There was a flash of red hair, and Aaron sat up in Mr. Rockefeller's bed. His laptop was in his lap.

"Where am I?" he said, looking everywhere except at Mr. Headbloom.

He snatched Aaron out and tried to remake the bed with a few quick moves of one hand. It was the best part of the whole field trip. Mr. Headbloom sprinted out of the exhibit and high-jumped the rope. He had Aaron by one arm. The laptop was swinging from Aaron's other hand. They both cleared the rope like champions. When they lit out in the hall, Mr. Headbloom was breathing hard.

This museum has no cafeteria. We had box lunches in an area with tables. I couldn't interface with Aaron because he had to sit next to Mr. Headbloom.

"I am still shocked, Zimmer," he said, "profoundly shocked."

"It was a project," Aaron said in a small, mouselike voice. "I was doing an I.S." Meaning Independent Study.

"Zimmer, we don't do I.S. until upper school. What you did was infantile. Preliterate. You were acting like . . ."

He was acting like Buster Brewster is what Mr. Headbloom meant. But teachers don't mention Buster's name lightly. Checking around for Buster myself, I saw him in the distance. He had a fourth grader up against a wall and was going through his backpack.

"Profoundly shocked," Mr. Headbloom said to Aaron again. But we were over the worst. At Huckley they don't call your parents unless you're in the actual hands of the law.

We decided to bypass the school bus and walk home that afternoon. We live thirty-some blocks south on Fifth. And it was a fairly mild day, January thaw or whatever.

Aaron strolled along, as normal as he gets.

"Zimmer, I'm shocked," I said. "Profoundly shocked."

"Knock it off, Josh. It was an independent study, like I told Headbloom."

"You were doing an independent study of Rockefeller's bed?" At the Eighty-sixth Street intersection I had to play crossing guard to keep Aaron from walking out into the traffic.

He sighed. "Look, I'm in early stages, but I'll try to explain."

"Do that."

"And I'll try to keep it simple."

"Appreciate it."

"You familiar with dark fiber?"

"Sure. What is it?"

"It's the part of fiber-optic cabling that isn't being used yet," Aaron said. "The data being beamed over fiber-optic networks is rising exponentially."

"What's that mean?"

"We're beaming a whole lot more data every minute. But only point one percent of fiber capacity is being used."

"Right."

"The rest is dark fiber."

"Okay."

"There's a strand in there somewhere that'll beam present-day people into the past. And probably back. I think it must be cellular reorganization."

"Says who?"

"It's my own theory. Hit the right digital frequency, and you'll experience physical translation."

"When do we get to Rockefeller's bed?"

"I've got my theory reduced to numbers that I'm satisfied with. And I've worked up some graphs. Did you know that the computer printer at school can do transparencies?"

"Hadn't noticed that," I said.

We strolled on down Fifth Avenue. And I wondered if Aaron was too weird to know. The elastic on one of his socks had given out. The sock drooped down over his shoe.

"It's more than an equation. It's all part of a larger internet," he said. "I haven't got it fine-tuned yet. It's like I'm one number off. It's like I'm shy one dark fiber. It's like I'm one channel away. It's like—"

"Okay, okay," I said. "I get your point."

"You know what I'm missing?" He elbowed my side. "It's something like the will or the need." He made a fist and looked at it. It was about half the size of Buster's. "I want it, but I don't want it enough. Something like that."

"Which means what?"

"The Emotional Component."

Emotional Component?

"It's not just what you know," Aaron said, "it's what you want. Maybe you can only get to the past if you really need to a lot."

Then it happened.

Four guys came out of Central Park a half block ahead. They were held up by a wagon train of city buses. Then they were crossing Fifth Avenue, giving cabs the finger.

Ball caps on backward. Black leather jackets. T-shirts down to their knees. Ripped Levi's. Two-hundred-dollar gym shoes. And eighth grade if not older. Trouble.

I was trying to remember what you're supposed to do. You're supposed to run out into traffic and take your chances against vehicles. But this bunch was already out there.

Then they spotted us. Aaron was still in his dream world of dark fiber and Emotional Component. I was screaming inside.

We were right in the middle of a block. No side street, nothing. There were a few people on the sidewalk. But they were all don't-get-involved types. Local people, and you're really safer with tourists.

The fearsome foursome was in the middle of Fifth Avenue and angling our way. They'd spotted us, and they'd talked us over. They'd probably even voted. Now they were heading for us, and they had public school written all over them. We were sitting ducks in Huckley dress code and still eleven blocks from home. Dead meat. You can count on your doorman, but not other people's.

I nudged Aaron, and for once this alerted him. "Yikes," he said. "Muggers to the fourth power."

Then he must have freaked out. He lifted one knee to balance his laptop. He flipped it open and started to type up something, an equation or formula or whatever. I had about ten seconds left to look cool. Then I had ball caps on all sides of me.

"Yo, preppy," a ball cap said in an already-changed voice.

I was worried about boxcutters. But all I saw now were big bunches of knuckles. The whole world turned black leather. And the first punch connecting with my head really unplugged my modem.

6

Aaron Up a Tree

When I came to, I felt a wet nose in my ear. At first I had thought it was my own nose. I thought maybe my face had been that rearranged. But out of the swelling eye on that side, I saw it was a French poodle in a plaid jacket. Its owner pulled it away and continued on uptown.

I was stretched on cold concrete. I hadn't been this flat-out since Fenella got us thrown out of that club. At least this was Fifth Avenue. My backpack had broken my fall, more or less. I could feel the shapes of books still in it. Somehow the killer quartet hadn't been too interested in books.

I only had about an eye and a half. Trying to move set off car alarms in my head. Aaron was crouching over me. "You okay?" he said.

"I been better. What did they get?"

"What did you have?"

"About four dollars and change."

"That's what they got. They didn't want your watch. They had Rolexes. You feel like moving?"

He was talking to me, but he was gazing around at Fifth Avenue. Maybe he was worried that the gang would circle back and zero in on us again.

My backpack weighed a ton, but I sat up. My nose was bleeding slightly on my shirt. When I looked down, I saw I had only half a Huckley tie left. It was sliced off just under the knot right through the dimple. So they did have boxcutters.

"You got a handkerchief?" I said.

"You kidding? Use your sleeve. This is an emergency." But still he kept gazing over his shoulder at the street, which was nothing but cabs racing to make the light. He wouldn't look me in the eye, and I only had one eye. I began to wonder about this. I looked him over. He had two eyes and a complete necktie, with traces of goat cheese.

"What did they get off you?"

"Nothing," he mumbled.

"Hey," I said, "why me?"

He shrugged.

"You telling me that they walked right past you to get me? You're smaller. They'd have gone right for you."

"They didn't see me," Aaron muttered.

"You're not that little."

"I wasn't here," he said, almost whispering.

"You didn't run," I said. They'd have brought him down in three paces.

"Not exactly. Let's see if you can stand up."

I had to make two trips, but I got there. I found my feet while heavy metal played in my head. My eye on the poodle side was now swollen shut. Aaron just stood there. He was sneaking peeks at the street, or across the street at the park.

"Let's go home," I said. "I can make it."

"In a minute." Now he was edging away, out to the curb.

"If you want a cab," I said, "you're paying."

But he wasn't looking for a cab. He was looking across at the trees in the park. He was so cyberspaced I thought about limping home by myself. Then he came back and gave me one of his owl looks.

"I was over there," he said, "up that tree, the third one down from the trash can."

"You were up in that tree while I was being pounded on?"

"In a sense."

"Wrong. You didn't have time to get there. You'd have to shoot across three lanes of traffic and two parking lanes before you even squirreled up a tree. You'd have been flattened."

"The traffic was already stopped before I even started across. They'd all hit their brakes. It was deafening."

"They'd stopped for my mugging?"

"No. There'd been sort of an accident down there, just past that manhole cover."

It made me look, one-eyed, out at Fifth. The cabs were flying by. There was no accident out there.

I told him that. "Aaron, *I'm* the accident. Do you see an accident out there?"

"Not now," he mumbled. "Not today."

My left eye felt like a paperweight. A bunch of people were line dancing in my head.

"It worked, Josh."

"What worked?"

"My equation. My formula." He held up his laptop. "It combined spontaneously with my need to escape. I was dark fibered into another time frame."

"And up a tree?"

"I've got some of my numbers wrong. Or something."

"Let's have this in layman's terms," I said. "You turned invisible to get away from that gang and, pow, you're up a tree and back in time?"

"Not exactly. I didn't turn invisible. I just suddenly wasn't here."

"I was. They nearly beat the—"

"And you weren't here either. I looked over from my tree, and you weren't here. Neither was the gang. And another thing. I didn't go back in time."

"Aaron, trust me. I never thought you could."

"I went forward."

My eye bored into him. "You went forward? Like into the future?"

He nodded. "I'm off on my numbers. I shouldn't even be trying anything like this on a laptop. It's going to need a new battery pack, at least."

"How far into the future do you think you went? Were there spaceships? Were there people here from other planets? Was the whole city climate-controlled under a dome? Was there trash collection?"

Aaron's eyes looked shifty. I may have looked bad, but he didn't look so good himself. Under the red hair his face was so pale that he looked like a radish. "Not that far," he said. "Maybe just a matter of days. A week or so."

"You mean everything looked the same?"

"More or less. It was still winter. You weren't here. You were probably someplace else that day. I probably was too. I didn't see us."

"Then how do you know it wasn't a few days *ago* instead of a few days *from now*?"

Aaron looked really worried. "Because of the accident."

I try to be skeptical. "Accidents happen every day on Fifth," I said. "Yesterday, today, tomorrow."

"Not this accident," he muttered.

"Like it was really bad? A big pileup or something?"

"It wasn't cars. It wasn't that kind of accident. Anyway, I wasn't there long enough. I was only gone about ninety seconds. What do you want from that, a miniseries?"

This was weird talk, even from Aaron. "So how'd you get back?"

"Well, I still had my laptop with me. I wedged it into that fork in the tree over there. I punched up my formula in reverse. Then I had these shooting pains all over my body. I'd had them before on the way out. That could have been my cells falling into place. Then I was right here on the sidewalk again, and you had a poodle in your ear."

"Aaron—"

"But I don't want to talk about it anymore now. I don't feel so good."

"*You* don't feel good? I probably need stitches."

He was already walking off down Fifth. I caught up with him and kept him in my good eye. At Seventy-ninth Street I had to hold him back to keep him from walking against the light. I'm still bleeding down my front, but I have to monitor him. If I hadn't been hurting so bad, I'd have been mad.

"Look, Aaron, I want to be on the record about something. I don't believe one word you—"

"I'm not going into the future anymore," he said. "It's too big a responsibility."

When I got home, the apartment felt empty. Aaron had gone on up to the penthouse. He had some major data-mining to do. He has a state-of-the-art, stand-alone microsystem workstation in his bedroom.

Mom wasn't home from Barnes Ogleby, and I kind of wished she was. I wanted to show her my eye and my nose and maybe cry a little.

Edging out of my backpack, I headed off to my

bathroom. At the door I heard a whirring sound. But my head was still whirring anyway. I opened the bathroom door. There was a piercing scream from inside.

Heather. In a bath towel. She'd been standing at my sink. In my mirror she caught a glimpse of my face. She whirled around and dropped her hair dryer, which stopped whirring. "What *happened* to you?"

"Why are you in my bathroom?" I said. "Why aren't you in your bathroom?"

"I always wash my hair in your bathroom. I don't want to get hair in my drain."

"Why didn't I know this?"

"You weren't supposed to. It's my business. What *happened* to you?"

"Mugged."

"What—getting off the school bus?"

"We didn't take the bus. We walked."

"You walked? What do you think the bus is *for*?" Heather smacked her forehead. "You are so immature. What happened to Pencil-Neck?"

Pencil-Neck is her name for Aaron. Don't ask me why.

"He . . . got away."

Heather tightened her towel and started wringing her hands. "Come on," she said. "We've got to clean you up before Mom gets home. Let me see that eye. Yewww. I'll get ice. You start washing. What happened to your tie?"

"Boxcutter."

I peeled out of my blazer and untied my stubby tie. Then I took a chance and looked in the mirror. I was pretty scary. My eye looked like it belonged to a giant frog. My nose had stopped bleeding, but there was a big clot on my lip. I grinned to see if I had all my teeth. I did. The blood came off, but the eye was looking worse. I dabbed around it with a soapy washcloth.

Heather was back with a bowl of ice. "Here, slap some of this on your eye."

"I'm not slapping anything near that eye."

"Give me that washcloth." She folded some cubes into it. "Take off your shirt. I'll soak it before the blood sets. Do I have to do everything? This is so typical of you, Josh. You never think a minute ahead. The future is a big blank space to you. What if Mom comes home and sees you like this? Think about it. You know how she overreacts. She'll start carrying on about how we're latchkey kids and need supervision. She'll be all over us. She thinks we're about four years old anyway. She'll want us in *day care*. And all because you're dumb enough to wander around getting mugged. She'll call Dad."

I hadn't thought about that.

"She'll lay a major guilt trip on him. He'll probably fly back here from Chicago." Now she was shaking a bloody shirt in my face.

"That would be okay," I said.

Heather sighed. "Josh, they've just separated. It's not time for a reconciliation. It's—*premature*. Don't you know anything about relationships? Don't you ever watch *Oprah*?"

She was running water to soak my shirt. "Oh, great," she said. "Your drain's clogged.

"And another thing. You know how Mom and Dad will see this, don't you? They'll think you managed this mugging as a cry for help."

"I didn't cry for help," I said. "They beat me senseless before I could open my mouth."

"Not that. They'll think you made this happen because of the separation. Like you're acting out because you're being single-parented. Mom'll take you for counseling. She'll take *me*. That eye is so gross."

Then Heather was gone. But she told me not to move. I wouldn't have minded an aspirin. But I just stood there. Then she was back with a bunch of stuff from Mom's makeup table.

"What's that for?"

"Your eye looks like an Easter egg. It won't heal for ages. I'm going to touch it up a little."

"Don't even think about coming near that eye."

"It's just a little Max Factor Erace creamy coverup. It's just a little pressed powder I can brush on."

But there was still some fight in me, and I fought her off.

That's when Mom appeared in the bathroom door. It took her a moment to see everything. The bloody shirt floating in the sink. The busted hair dryer on the floor. Heather bath toweled with half-dried hair. Me shirtless and fighting her off as she tried to revise my face with Mom's own Max Factor and Estée Lauder products.

Then she got a good view of my Easter-egg eye. Mom's hand clamped over her mouth to stifle a scream.

7

No Seat, No Hands

"All right," Mom sighed, "let's try to put our best feet forward."

We were in a cab again, heading out to JFK Airport. Mom was giving Au Pair Exchange another shot, and we had another plane to meet.

"I can't be in two places," Mom said, "and there can't be two Fenellas."

A week had passed. Now I just had a black eye. Mom could look at me without bursting into tears.

"Okay," Heather moaned. "Who's it going to be this time?"

"Feona," Mom said, trying to sound confident.

According to the Au Pair Exchange printout, Feona was seventeen, a recent "school leaver," whose interests were

reading
field hockey
gardening
needlework
flower arranging
gourmet cooking
and equitation

"What's equitation supposed to be?" Heather asked.

"Horseback riding," Mom said.

There was a dim Xerox picture of Feona in a school uniform and straw hat. It didn't look too recent and could have been anybody.

There was the usual business about Feona assisting with light household work, food preparation, and child care, twenty hours a week tops.

"I don't like her already," Heather said as we pulled up to the British Air terminal. "And if her plane's late, I'm going home in a cab by myself. Camilla Van Allen might call."

"She's never called yet," I muttered.

"Mo-om," Heather said, "make Josh put a sock in it or I'll have to go to boarding school."

When they announced the flight from London, the first passenger out of the Customs door was this girl. She was pretty tall, with long red cheeks and plenty of teeth. Her hair was pulled back in a ponytail. She was wearing a tweed jacket, riding pants, and spit-shined high boots. You couldn't miss her. She was carrying a saddle.

"Who's this?" Heather said. "My friend Flicka?"

"Feona?" Mom said, because the girl was looking around, maybe for a horse.

"Actually, yes," Feona said. "Brilliant to meet you." She propped her saddle under one arm to shake hands with all three of us. "Absolutely brill." She had a bone-crusher grip.

"You'd make a super jockey," she said down to me, "if you don't get any bigger."

"I'm Josh," I said in a short voice. "Want me to carry your saddle?" I hoped not. It was bigger than I was.

"Thanks awfully. I'm never without it. But you're an absolute poppet to ask," Feona said.

Fenella had called me Tiny Tim. Feona called me a poppet. It was like a whole different language.

She turned to Heather. Expecting another Fenella, Heather had punked out. She was in total black except her lips, which Mom wouldn't let her do.

"Feona, actually," Feona said. She lifted Heather's hand from her side and gave it a bone-crusher. "How's your seat?"

"My *what*?" Heather said.

"No seat, no hands, Daddy always says," Feona said to Mom.

"Ah," Mom said. "And what would that mean . . . actually?"

Feona stared. "If you don't sit a horse well, you'll never handle the reins well. No seat, no hands."

"Ah," Mom said.

"I've got a pain in my seat," Heather muttered. "And I know who's caused it."

Outside, Heather and I were the last ones into the cab. Heather turned back to me. "She even smells weird. Do you know what it is?"

"Horse," I said.

"That's the first syllable," Heather said.

The saddle had to go into the trunk, which Feona wasn't too happy about. The four of us were bunched in the backseat. I was practically on the floor. It was dark, but you could see that every time Feona moved, her ponytail swatted Heather in the face. Heather was bobbing and weaving, trying to keep hair out of her mouth.

". . . I hope you'll be—comfortable with us," Mom said. I could read her mind. At least Feona wasn't another Fenella.

"Oh, I'm quite comfortable anywhere," Feona said. "My school didn't have heat."

"Ah," Mom said. "I suppose that would be boarding school?"

Feona twitched her tail. "We go away to school when we're seven. It's super, really. You meet such a lot of jolly girls. And it lets your parents get on with their marriage."

"Ah," Mom said.

"Actually, at school, I slept most nights with Cheeky Bob in the stables."

"Cheeky Bob?" Mom said doubtfully.

"My horse, of course. We're about to put him out at stud. All the mares are mad for him."

Heather looked around her at me.

"I'm really just a bumper in the saddle," Feona confided. "And I'm better on the flat than at the fence. But I'm dead keen. And it's brill being here. I'm only missing the first of the point-to-points. Absolutely riveting, but filthy weather for it."

"Point-to-point?" Mom said.

Feona stared again. "It's a race like a steeplechase. But the jumps are six inches lower. Surely you have them? Mummy brings a hamper and we have picnics. Absolutely br—"

"Then it's not a hunt," Mom said. "You don't kill animals."

"No," Feona explained. "That's later in the season."

Now the whole cab smelled like a stable. Up front, the cabby was spraying his area with an aerosol can.

We gunned along the expressway. It was another one of those nights when you get that great view of the city. Twinkling towers, chains of lights on the bridges. That type of thing.

Feona leaned forward, whisking Heather. "Whatever is that?" She pointed through the bullet-proof Plexiglas and over the cabby's shoulder.

"That's Manhattan," I told her. "The Big Apple."

Feona blinked. "But whyever is it getting nearer and nearer?"

"We *live* there," Heather said.

Feona fell back in the seat. "There's been some mistake," she said to Mom. "Au Pair Exchange said you lived in the country. They said you kept horses. They said you were deeply committed to stalking and shooting. They said you had some jolly good coverts."

"Coverts?" Mom murmured.

Feona sighed. "Places where the fox hides."

"There's a lot of stalking and shooting in Manhattan," I said. "But we don't do it."

Mom was tensing up. "Au Pair Exchange said you liked flower arranging," she said to Feona.

"Me? You mean weeds and grasses in pots? Mummy does that."

Mom clutched her purse with both hands. "I'll kill those Au Pair Exchange people," she said. "I'll find out who they are. I'll get a gun. I'll track them down. I'll flush them out of their coverts. And I'll kill them."

8

Alone in the Black Hole

School's not that much fun without your best friend. Aaron had made himself scarce ever since my mugging day. For over a week he'd been signing himself out of classes to work at the terminals in the Black Hole. He went in early and stayed after school, so I didn't see him on the bus. He was in there at lunch.

Then, whenever I did run into him, he'd say, "I'm still diddling my data." And he'd be off to the Black Hole again like he didn't have time for me.

At first I thought he might be mad. He knew I didn't believe he'd time-warped himself up a tree for my mugging. I try to be skeptical, but this time it might have hurt his feelings.

Then one day in the school lunchroom I was down at the end of a table eating a lonely burrito. Aaron comes in, scanning around to see where I am.

Huckley School is built in a row of four old houses put together. They flattened one roof and fenced it in for the lower-school playground. Otherwise they've tried to keep the houses pretty much the way they were. They even named them for the families who lived in them years ago. The lunchroom is the old dining room of Havemeyer House. It's decorated with hockey sticks and pictures of past lacrosse teams and old Havemeyers.

Aaron spotted me. He worked his way through the crowd, carrying a lunch off the salad bar. He dropped down beside me.

"Getting there," he said like the old Aaron. So maybe he wasn't mad at me. He probably wasn't. "Like I said, I was off on my numbers. Also, I can do better work on the terminals here at school. How far did I think I was going to get on a one-chip laptop? And at school I can work on two computers. This could be the evolutionary reason why we have two hands. With two on-line databases, you can practically conduct a symphony."

So it was definitely the old Aaron.

"I'm making progress," he said, "but it's not all a matter of direct data entry."

"Wouldn't be," I said.

"There's the Emotional Component."

"After all, the human brain is the ultimate computer," I reminded him.

"But if it means scaring myself into some other time," Aaron said, "I'm up for it. I'll jump that fence when I come to it."

Jumping fences reminded me of horses. Horses reminded me of you know who.

"We've got another O Pear," I said.

But Aaron wasn't listening. For once he didn't have his one-chip laptop with him. But the fingers of his left hand were punching up something on the bare wood of the lunch table. Once in a while his fork would come up, and he'd stuff lettuce in his mouth. But his eyes were unfocused, and his mind was way off somewhere. There was a blob of Thousand Island dressing on his nose.

This began to make me mad. It happens a lot. Right after you think your best friend is mad at you, and then you find he isn't, you get mad at him. Aaron was taking himself too seriously. He was getting weirder. He was beginning to buy his own theories. I thought about turning him in to the counseling office. He wouldn't even notice if I got up and walked away.

Then he got up and walked away. He wandered through the lunchroom crowd, returned his empty salad bowl, and left in the direction of the media center.

I had a little bit of burrito left but didn't even feel like eating it.

After school I was getting on the bus with the rest of the backpackers. I was going with the flow. Then I turned around and went back into school. Having to find a new best friend at my age is just too big a deal.

The media center is in Vanderwhitney House, a couple of buildings over from Havemeyer House. It was probably the personal library of the Vanderwhitney family in the olden days. Some of the shelves are real wood built into the walls.

The front part of it still has some books. Mrs. Newbery, the media specialist, was giving a story hour there to a bunch of preschoolers in miniature dress code. The back part is walled off with a door in it, and that's the Black Hole where the computer workstations are.

Aaron was in there, positioned between two terminals. He was keeping them busy with both hands. All the compartments of his brain were fully engaged.

I just stood there. What are you going to do with a kid like that? I couldn't see his face, but I knew his lips were moving. Then I got this idea. It was a spur-of-the-moment thing. If Aaron's so sure he can be scared into another time frame, let's find out.

I closed the door behind me to keep Mrs. Newbery from being involved. Then I made a dead run for Aaron. I came pounding up on his blind side.

"Aaron, look out! Buster Brewster's got a gun, and he's heading this way!"

Aaron froze. Then he yelled, "Yikes!" His hands flew up. He was surrendering or something. Then his hands dropped down on both keyboards. His fingers flew. The entire Black Hole seemed to give out a glow. It was like a power surge.

Then the scariest thing that ever happened, happened.

Something was happening to Aaron. He was beginning to . . . dim. He was like somebody fading into the distance, except he was right here—a reach away. I didn't know whether to touch him or not, but I put one hand out on his bony shoulder. It was changing under my hand. It felt like a Baggie full of bees. This could have been his cells reorganizing themselves. I think I even heard buzzing, but that could have been the terminals.

Then my hand was just there, hanging in space. I was standing behind an empty chair. Aaron was lost in cyberspace.

I panicked. Who wouldn't? I checked under the terminals, in the corners, even. But I was alone in the Black Hole. Through the wall I could hear the drone of Mrs. Newbery's voice, summing up a story.

If Aaron will just get his tail back here, I'll never doubt him again, I was screaming inside. Did he have his laptop with him? Could he program himself back from wherever? Will I be held responsible for this? I looked at both screens. They were blank.

Time passed. I don't know how long. Something had gone wrong with time. The door opened behind me. If it had been Buster Brewster with a gun, I'd have had it coming. It was Mrs. Newbery.

"Oh, Josh," she said. "I thought it was Aaron in here. It usually is. Brushing up on your computer literacy?"

But then she looked over my shoulder at the terminals. Across both blank screens words were spelling themselves out:

HARD DRIVE FAILURE

9

Aaron Zimmer Is Missing

I had to leave. Mrs. Newbery was closing up for the night, and what could I tell her? Then I was drifting down Fifth Avenue in a fog all my own. I even walked right past my mugging site without flinching.

What was I supposed to do, call the police to put out an all-points for Aaron? They'd drag the rivers, and I was almost a hundred percent sure he wasn't there. Was I supposed to put up laser printouts on lampposts?

AARON ZIMMER IS MISSING
Undersized crazed redhead in Huckley dress code
swallowed by two hostile computers

Please.

Then I was home, fighting my way out of my backpack. Then I went into action. In my room I punched up the Zimmer penthouse on my phone. Nobody knows the native language of the Zimmers' housekeeper. But she speaks four words of English: "hello," "say what?" and "okay."

"Hello," she said.

"This is Josh down on twelve. Aaron is . . . here. He wants to spend the night. We're . . . going to put up a tent and camp out in the living room."

Nobody older than third grade would do that. But it was all I could think of. "Can Aaron sleep over?"

"Say what?"

I repeated the message. "This is Josh down on twelve. Aaron is . . ." etc.

The housekeeper said, "Okay," and hung up.

This bought me some time. But so what? Maybe Aaron wouldn't be back. Maybe he wasn't . . . bidirectional. I didn't even want to think about going to school tomorrow. But then, I mainly think about what's happening now. I'd jump that fence when I got to it.

I was just collapsing my phone aerial when my bedroom door burst open.

Heather.

She shrieked and clutched her head. "Get off that phone!"

"Why should I? It's mine. Use your own phone."

"But I give out your number." She snatched the phone out of my hand.

"Give out your own number," I said.

"I do. I give out both. I might be getting two calls."

"We have call waiting."

"I know that. But giving out two numbers makes our apartment sound bigger."

"Why didn't I know you were giving out my number?"

"You weren't supposed to. It's my business." She was patting my phone like a Barbie doll. Now she was in my face, whispering. "You'll never guess who's here."

"Feona?"

"Of course Feona's here. Guess who else."

But I was out of guesses.

"Camilla Van Allen." Heather can squeal and whisper at the same time.

"Great," I said. "So you're in the peer group finally?"

Heather did a dance with my phone as her partner. "It's like a miracle."

"So if Camilla Van Allen is here—"

"She is. She's right in this apartment. As we speak. In the living room with Feona. We're having English tea. With cucumber sandwiches. Camilla loves it. Her grandmother is English."

"Great. So if Camilla's here, why do I have to keep off my phone?"

"Josh, you are so immature. Think. Now that I'm in with Camilla, everybody will be calling." Heather did six more dance steps toward the door and left, taking my phone.

Then she was back, handing me my phone.

"Listen, if I get a call, take a message. Stay in your room. You don't need to meet Camilla. I don't want anything to go wrong. Are there any questions?"

"Look, Heather, I've got a lot on my mind," I said. "Maybe you could just tell me why Camilla Van Allen is here and what it has to do with Feona. Keep it short. I thought you didn't like Feona. You said she smelled like horse—"

"But I remembered that Camilla Van Allen's family has a horse farm in Far Hills. Feona's on Camilla's social level, but English. She rides. She's going to teach me to ride. I'm going to get a good seat. Camilla will invite me to Far Hills. What am I going to wear? I happened to mention Feona in school where Camilla could hear. I didn't say Feona was an O Pear, for heaven's sake. I said she was like related to us. Do you know what her last name is?"

"Didn't catch it."

"Foxworthy," Heather breathed.

Feona Foxworthy?

"The Foxworthys are practically royalty. Their name rang a bell with Camilla. Feona's family lives in two places: London and their country estate."

"Our mom and dad live in two places. New York and Chi—"

"Not like that."

"I thought Feona wasn't staying. She thought we had stables and horses. She thought we stalk and shoot."

"But we've got Central Park. Camilla's telling her how you can rent horses from a stable over on West Eighty-ninth Street."

"Great," I said. "Brill." But Heather was out the door.

When I was sure she was gone, I punched the Zimmer penthouse number again, just to be on the safe side. I told their housekeeper that Aaron and I would leave from here for school tomorrow. I'd loan him a clean shirt and underwear.

"Say what?" she said. I repeated myself. She said okay.

When I signed off, the phone rang. "Hello," said this voice. "This is Muffie MacInteer. Is Camilla Van Allen there?"

I took a message. The next day I had to go back to school. And Aaron wasn't going to be on the bus.

10

To Horse and Away

Feona was an early riser. I had a quick breakfast with her. She wore her velvet riding hard hat at the table and was reading a magazine called *Horse and Hound.* She sort of fed and watered herself.

I was at school by seven-thirty. The media center in Vanderwhitney House wasn't officially open yet, but it was unlocked. I crept past the books back to the Black Hole. That door was locked.

The situation looked hopeless. My head hurt from worrying. I rested it against the door.

A voice spoke from the other side. "Mrs. Newbery?" A familiar voice.

"Aaron?"

"Josh?"

Now I was annoyed. I practically hadn't slept all night. Now this.

"Get the key," the small voice said. "It's in Mrs. Newbery's top left-hand desk drawer. Under her bottle of Maalox."

I went for it and got lucky. Mrs. Newbery didn't come in to find me rifling through her desk. She was due any minute.

When I opened the door, Aaron was standing there in yesterday's clothes. Red rims circled his eyes. He was eating an apple. He looked around me.

"You were just kidding about Buster Brewster and a gun, right?"

I sighed. "Aaron—"

He put up a small hand. "Josh, it's too late for skeptical. You were there. And then I wasn't. Right? You can't deny it."

"But I didn't see anything. You were gone. And where did you get that apple anyway?"

"It was in a big silver bowl of fruit over there on a table."

"Aaron, I don't see a big silver bowl of fruit. I don't see a table."

"Not now," he said. "Then."

He strolled over to the terminals. He'd shut them down. They were blank-screened and cold. "Let me show you how I did it. Two keyboards helped. I entered half the formula on this one, half on that one. It set up a real matrix."

"So what is this formula anyway?" I said.

His red eyes peered up at me. "It's a forty-eight-character combination of numbers and letters, clustered. With some visuals."

"Ah," I said. "Right."

"Josh, why tell it to you? It took you till third grade to remember your zip code."

"Rub it in," I said.

"And I'm not writing it down," he said. "This could be dangerous information in the wrong hands. I'm keeping it up here." He tapped his temple. "The human brain—"

"Is the ultimate computer," I said. "Aaron, I'm doing my best, but I still can't buy in. Numbers on a screen, clustered. Visuals. The whole forty-eight-character ball of wax. But how does it get you . . . there?"

Aaron looked a little worn, like a teacher after seventh period.

"Let me give you a metaphor, Josh. It's the best I can do. You can fax a letter, right? You can fax a document, right? You can fax a photo, right?" He dropped his voice even lower. "Josh, you can fax yourself."

I stared.

"You helped," he said. "You scared me about Buster. You gave me the boost. Adrenaline is a definite factor. I just lined up my numbers with my need and . . . went."

"But you didn't have your laptop with you. How did you get back without entering your formula or whatever?"

"Good point," Aaron said. "Important point. I didn't have to. I hadn't needed it the other day up that tree in Central Park. Cellular reorganization is a temporary condition. In layman's terms, when your time's up, you're back. It's fairly painful both ways."

"So you're—"

"That's right," Aaron said. "I'm bidirectional."

I stood there, trying to stare him down, trying to see into his quirky brain. Skeptical dies hard.

"How long were you gone?"

"Not long," he said. "Minutes. Then I was back. But I was locked in here for the night. I had to sleep on the floor."

"I covered for you," I said. "I told your housekeeper you were sleeping over. I told her we were putting up a tent in my living room."

"Nobody older than third grade does that," he said. "Couldn't you think of anything better?"

Which was the thanks I got.

"Okay, Aaron. Let's get down to basics. Where did you go?"

His eyes shifted away from mine. He'd nibbled his apple down to the core. Also, he probably had to go to the bathroom. "Zero distance," he muttered.

"Meaning you weren't up a tree again?"

"I was right here in this room. But it was then, not now. Way back then."

"Aaron. When?"

"Put it this way," he said. "I've just eaten an apple that I estimate to be about seventy-five years old." He showed me the core.

A shadow fell over us. A voice spoke. "Are you boys losing track of time?"

It was Mrs. Newbery in the doorway. We jumped. "You've practically missed Mr. Headbloom's homeroom," she said. "If you don't cut along, you'll be late for Linear Decoding." We started to cut along.

"I'll take my key if you don't mind." Mrs. Newbery put her hand out. Then she said to Aaron, "Better tidy up before you go to class. You look like you've slept in those clothes."

In Linear Decoding, Aaron was sitting across the room from me. We were reading *The Time Machine* by H. G. Wells, a dead English writer. I didn't see Aaron in Science or Gym. I didn't see him at lunch. He'd be diddling his data again.

This gave me time to get skeptical again. True, he'd vanished before my eyes. But it could have been an . . . optical illusion. He could have been messing with my mind.

After school he turned up and said, "Let's walk home."

"What about muggers?"

"Muggers, shmuggers," Aaron said. "I haven't been outdoors since yesterday morning. I could use some air."

As we turned down Fifth Avenue, I decided not to ask him anything. If this whole thing was a scam, I didn't want to fall for it. Then I couldn't think of anything to talk about. We trudged along for a few blocks. Aaron sticks his feet out funny when he walks.

At the Eighty-sixth Street light I said, "We've got another O Pear."

"Tell me about it, Josh." But he was listening with only half an ear.

"She's different from Fenella. Way different. Her name's Feona Foxworthy. She's okay, I guess. The funny thing is, Heather likes her."

Aaron froze. "Heather?" He doesn't have that much of a relationship with Heather. And she calls him Pencil-Neck.

"Feona got Heather into Camilla Van Allen's peer group, so Heather likes her. Feona's horsey."

Aaron quivered. He pulled on his chin in a thoughtful, weird way. "Tall girl? Long face? Plenty of teeth? Ponytail? Riding hat?"

"That's her. You see her on the elevator or someplace?"

"Someplace," he said. "Where are they now?" His hand was closing over my arm.

"Heather and Feona?" I said. "Who knows?"

"Yikes," Aaron said. "This could be the *day*." He was so hyper, he was almost doing a dance.

He started running down Fifth, dragging me along. I didn't know he could move that fast. He should go out for track instead of always signing himself out of Gym.

"Where are we going?" I gasped. But he was saving his breath. We almost vaulted the hood of a cab at Eighty-second.

"Whoa," I said at the light on Seventy-ninth, which has traffic both ways. But he was jogging in place and breathing hard. He was stretching his neck to see down Fifth Avenue.

He wouldn't wait for the light to change. He made an end run around a crosstown bus, stopping a van in its tracks. Then we were streaking down the sidewalk again, coming up on my mugging site. Yellow cabs flowed south, and we almost kept up with them.

Then it was like the world stopped. All the cabs screeched to a halt. So did Aaron. So did I. Cabbies leaned on their horns. Metal crunched from a couple of fender-benders behind us. The cabbies were rolling down their windows and yelling in every language but English.

"Too late," Aaron said. "And we were *this close*."

The cabs weren't going anywhere now. He darted out and sprinted between them down Fifth Avenue. Then we got there.

Two horses—big ones—were in the middle of the street. One was reared up with its hooves fighting the air. Our O Pear, Feona Foxworthy, was on it. One of her boots was out of the stirrup. Her riding hat was slipping off. She'd lost the reins and had the horse's neck in a death grip. "Daddy!" Feona shrieked. "Mummy!"

The other horse was stamping on Fifth Avenue pavement, and its eyes were rolling. Connected to it by a rein was Heather. She was stretched out in the middle of the street in a new top-of-the-line riding outfit: velvet hard hat, tweed coat, riding pants, and boots. Some gray snow was sticking to her, so she must have been thrown off in the park and dragged here into traffic. You could tell the horse didn't like her.

A cop and a couple of cabbies were trying to talk Feona's horse down. And they were getting between Heather and her horse to keep it from kicking her in the head.

Heather was gazing glassy-eyed into the winter sky with one arm up because of the rein. The cop and the cabbies were trying to untangle her. But she must have been stunned because she yelled, " 'Ere, stand aside, you miserable gits." Then just as Aaron and I got up to her, she fainted, or seemed to.

"Too late," Aaron said again. "This is the future I saw from my tree the other day when my numbers were a little off. This was the accident."

"Whoa, Aaron," I said. Heather's horse looked at me.

"But I guess we couldn't have headed off the accident anyway." Aaron gave a helpless shrug. "I couldn't even believe it was Heather at the time. That riding outfit's new, right? She'd never been on a horse before, right?"

"This looks like her first lesson," I said.

"This was the future I cellular-reorganized into, Josh. I saw all this happen more than a week ago. I was up that tree." He pointed into bare branches.

"You're not up there."

"Not now. I left before we got here. I left while Heather's horse was just dragging her over the curb into traffic. I didn't know who the other girl was."

"Mummy!" Feona was still shrieking as she slid down the side of her horse, or its flank or whatever. "Daddy!"

"Aaron—"

"I'm not going into the future anymore," he said. "Like I said, it's too big a responsibility. I'm going to stick with going back into the past."

11

A Tasteful Private Residence

Mom said, "Feona goes," and she went, that night.

The last we saw of her, she was lugging her saddle onto a British Air flight. She looked back and gave us a big toothy smile from under her velvet hard hat. "Do write!" she called out. Then she galloped onto the plane.

In the cab back to the city Mom sat with her eyes closed for a while.

"I am getting very near the end of my rope," she said.

I knew we were going to have to go over it again, even though we'd been over everything already. Heather stared out the window.

"Fenella tried to smuggle you into that *crack house* club where you might have been drugged for life or arrested. Or both. And the two of you followed along like a pair of geese. And Feona was worse. She was practically homicidal. Heather, what was your first mistake?" Mom waited.

"The riding clothes," Heather said in a sulky, mouselike voice. "On your credit card."

"I haven't even had my first paycheck from Barnes Ogleby," Mom said. "And you can't take them back to the store, not after that wild horse—that mustang—dragged you over half of Manhattan Island. *And* you cut school."

"Feona said it was the same as school," Heather mumbled. "At her school, riding lessons are part of the curriculum."

"That awful girl was all talk. She could have used a few more riding lessons herself. She must have fallen off her horse too often. On her head," Mom said. "*How's your seat*, my foot. I've come to the conclusion that Au Pair Exchange is a criminal outfit. I'm thinking about reporting them to the Better Business Bureau. I blame myself there."

If Heather was taking most of the heat and Mom blamed herself, I figured I could relax.

"And by the way, Josh," Mom said. "I ran into Mrs. Zimmer in the lobby. She wanted to thank us for having Aaron sleep over. I really didn't know what to say since I don't recall Aaron sleeping over. When you can come up with a good explanation for that, I'll be glad to hear it."

I sank lower in the seat and passed up that great nighttime view of Manhattan: twinkling towers, lit-up bridges. But I had a lot on my mind. Usually I think about now. But I was hung up between the future and the past that night. Way hung up.

At school the next day Aaron was in and out of class all morning. He's usually in business for himself, but today he was really hustling. He was late for Mr. Headbloom's Linear Decoding. Swinging past my desk, he dropped a sheet of paper on my copy of *The Time Machine*. It was a Xeroxed page from an old *New York Times*. It was black and white and blotchy, but I could read it.

A dim picture showed the Vanderwhitney House part of the school when it was brand-new:

Tasteful Residence of
the Osgood Vanderwhitneys

Distinctive New Home
for Distinguished Old Family

> Architects acclaim this residence of Mr. and Mrs. Osgood Vanderwhitney as the most tasteful private domicile to be built in the city during 1921. It features thirty rooms lavishly paneled and commodious accommodations for servants under a bronze dormer.
>
> The house, only steps from the Central Park, is the last to be built in a street already home to such prominent families as the Havemeyers, the Van Allens, and the Huckleys.
>
> After summering at Tuxedo Park, the Osgood Vanderwhitneys will reside here, along with their

two small sons, Cuthbert Henry, aged seven, and
Lysander Theodore, aged three.

Cuthbert Henry and Lysander Theodore?
At the bottom of the sheet Aaron had written:

House looked new when I was there but not this new.

This must mean he thought he'd cellular-reorganized back to the early days of the Vanderwhitneys' house. I missed him at lunch. He was late again for History. When he bustled in, he dropped another Xerox copy on me on the way to his desk.

"Zimmer. Freeze," Mr. Thaw said. He's Huckley's hardest teacher and the oldest. He should have retired long ago and gone to the Old Teachers' Home. "Number one," he said to Aaron, "you're late. Number two, you're passing notes. These are both misdemeanors in this class."

Aaron blinked.

"I'm doing an independent study," he squeaked.

"Zimmer, we don't do I.S. until—"

"I know," Aaron said, "but this is about the history of the school. Josh Lewis and I are putting together a program on it for Parents' Night."

This was quick thinking. But why drag me into it?

Huckley teachers are pretty careful about parents. Even crusty old Mr. L. T. Thaw. He stroked his straggly beard.

"Very well, Zimmer," he said, after giving it some thought. "I'll follow up to make sure that you and young Lewis make a presentation on Parents' Night. And make it good. The grades of both of you will depend upon it."

Thanks a lot, Aaron, I thought.

Mr. Thaw went back to the lesson. We were reading up on the presidents of the United States. At least Mr. Thaw was. He could probably remember most of them personally.

I had time to glance over Aaron's latest Xerox copy. It was a clipping from a 1923 *New York Times*:

Hook and Ladder Company Called to Fashionable Address

> The fire brigade answered an alarm from the home of the Osgood Vanderwhitneys on the smart Upper East Side at 3:30 P.M. yesterday. A fire of unknown origin in the library of the palatial townhouse threatened the lives of the two Vanderwhitney children, Cuthbert, aged nine, and Lysander, aged five.
>
> When New York's stalwart fire fighters arrived, the blaze had been extinguished. Damage was limited to a scorched bookshelf and the collected speeches of President Buchanan. Mr. Vanderwhitney was summoned from his Wall Street office. Mrs. Vanderwhitney is said to be en route from the family's Tuxedo Park country address.
>
> " 'All's Well That Ends Well,' " Mr. Vanderwhitney remarked, quoting Shakespeare.

Underneath, Aaron had put in a giant exclamation mark and a message:

Meet me after school in the Black Hole.
I'm going back. I've got enough Emotional
Component to send myself to the moon.

Nobody was around as I slipped through the media center. There were afternoon shadows everywhere. At first I thought Aaron wasn't in the Black Hole. The only thing I noticed was a big metal frame where they store manuals, floppy disks, and back issues of *Byte*. It was pulled out from the wall.

Down in the corner I saw a flash of red. Aaron stood up. "Shut the door behind you and come over here, Josh." Behind the metal frame were the original built-in shelves of the Vanderwhitney family's library. They were carved all around with wooden flowers, way too fragile to stand up to school use. "Look right there."

Some of the wood was darker than the rest, like flames might have licked up it long ago.

"Like the newspaper said."

"But it doesn't prove you went back there, Aaron."

"No, but I did. And it was around that time. About 1923. It could have been before the fire, or after. But I was there."

"Okay, what was this room like?" I said. "We've already heard about the table with the silver fruit bowl."

"It was where the terminals are now. The wall between here and the media center wasn't there, of course. It was one long room. It was nice. Polished wood floors, not this crummy tile. Big vases of flowers were standing around."

"Did they have electricity?"

"Of course they had electricity. It was 1923. And they were rich. But the lights weren't on. It was this time of day, more or less. Afternoon light was coming in that window."

"What window?"

"It was right there. They must have bricked it up when that big apartment building was built between here and Fifth Avenue." His voice trailed away.

"That's it?"

"I was only there for a few minutes. What do you want from that, a mini—"

"Was anybody in the room?"

He looked shifty and worried. "A couple of people," he murmured. "They were kissing. It was kind of embarrassing."

Kissing?

"Kissing each other?"

"Of course they were kissing each other. What else? She'd been crying. She took a handkerchief out of her sleeve and dabbed her eyes. The guy kept looking over his shoulder. They were both worried, like they might get caught. He had his arms around her, and they were whispering and kissing."

"That's it?"

"The girl reached inside the collar of her dress and pulled up a gold chain with a ring on it. Maybe he'd given her the ring, and she was wearing it around her neck, hiding it."

"Did they see you? Were you visible?"

"I don't know. They were kind of busy."

"Then what?" I was watching him closely.

"I stood there a while, just hanging around. Then I wanted to see if I could pick up an apple. I could. I was really there. Then I felt myself coming back. I was kind of embarrassed by all that kissing. So then I had shooting pains, that type of thing, and left."

The Black Hole was quiet. I wanted to go home now. "Aaron, it wouldn't hold up in court."

"I've got some more work to do on my formula. I'm still flying blind. I want some more control."

"Well," I said, "these things take—time."

Aaron had me about half-psyched again. And I was really ready to go home. We'd missed the bus, but we could walk. We both needed the air. Muggers, shmuggers.

But he was going into action mode again. Now he positioned himself between the two terminals. "You stand behind me, Josh. Put your hands on my shoulders so I'll know you're right there. I'm going to try to go back without Emotional Component, so don't try to scare me or anything. Just be there."

Already his hands were reaching for the keyboards.

"Wait a minute, Aaron."

"What for? I said I was going back, and I am. I'm going to try the same formula again. Later I'll diddle my data and fiddle my figures. For now I want you here. Mrs. Newbery is liable to turn up any minute."

"Let's say she finds me here in the room alone," I said. "She'll throw me out and lock up as usual."

"Then find a way of getting back in to spring me," Aaron said. "Use your initiative."

"But what if you don't—"

"Enough talk," Aaron said. His fingers splayed out over the two keyboards. Both my hands dropped on his bony shoulders. Maybe I could even hold him back. The formula unfurled like a flag of hot letters across both screens.

But Aaron's shoulders didn't feel like a Baggie full of bees this time, though I heard buzzing. Instead, pain like I'd never felt raced up my fingers, and along my arms, and burst like a blown fuse in my brain.

My mind raged and reorganized. I realized Aaron was entering the past. And I was going with him.

12

Thousands of Afternoons Ago

We whirled through time without moving. I smelled something frying and hoped it wasn't us. The whole experience hurt worse than my mugging. Then we fell over backward. Me being there probably threw us off balance. We landed on a polished wood floor.

We were behind a carved table. The first thing I saw was the ceiling. It had fancy plasterwork now—then. And a tinkling chandelier.

I was still clinging like a monkey to Aaron's back. He jerked around. "What are you *doing* here?"

I blinked.

"You must have been in my force field," he muttered.

Then we heard screaming.

We scrambled up in a crouch and peered over the table past a silver fruit bowl. There were two kids there: boys.

One was about nine or an overweight eight. He was wearing a full Indian costume: buckskin breeches, war paint over his freckles, feather headdress, and beaded moccasins. He had a tomahawk in his hand, and it looked like the real thing.

He was doing a war dance around a chair in the middle of the room. A smaller kid was tied to the chair by a lot of rope. Half the screams were his. The other half were the big one's war whoops.

"That is one hyperactive Native American," Aaron said.

It must have been Cuthbert in costume. Lysander was trussed up like a turkey in the chair and screaming his head off. Then I noticed the crumpled-up newspaper around the chair legs.

My head was aching anyway, and the screaming and whooping didn't help. I still had Aaron in a near-death grip.

Then Cuthbert dropped his tomahawk, reached down into his buckskin breeches, and came up with a box of matches. Before you could think, he struck a light. You could smell sulfur. A breeze from the window that was there then sent the lace curtains billowing. The flame jumped onto them. But Cuthbert was too focused to notice. He leaned down and set the crumpled paper on fire under Lysander's kicking feet.

Flames licked up the curtains. More flames started licking Lysander's feet. Luckily he was wearing buttoned-up high-tops.

Aaron and I leaped up and skidded around the table.

Little oriental rugs skittered under our feet. Cuthbert went on with his authentic war dance, waving his tomahawk around. Smoke drifted around the room, and Lysander was really yowling.

I didn't know what to do. "Quick," Aaron said. "Get a vase." There were flowers in glass vases around the long room. He grabbed one off a reading table, dumping out the flowers. Then he doused the burning paper under Lysander.

"Hey, no fair," Cuthbert said. We were visible, and he was annoyed. But he didn't seem that surprised to see us. He was probably used to having a lot of servants around. And by the way, where were they?

The lace curtains were going up like dry weeds. There was a fireplace on that wall. Two vases of flowers were up on the mantel. I went for one and could just reach it. I dumped the flowers and ran over to the window. The curtains were gone, but the flames had jumped to the bookcase. When the fire hit shellac, it went wild and spread over the books. I let fly with a vase full of water. Aaron came up with another. We were both breathing hard. I wasn't sure the bookcase was doused, but we were out of vases. Flowers were everywhere.

"Who do you think you are?" came Cuthbert's voice behind us.

"Untie me at once!" Lysander howled in a higher voice. But he was all tied up and too busy screaming to notice us.

Aaron and I stood there panting. Then we heard footsteps running down a hall that isn't there now. A big double door began to open. We whirled around, but I was having shooting pains all over like you can't believe. I reached out for Aaron, and his shoulder felt like a Baggie full of bees. We heard buzzing and a voice, but I blacked out for a moment. Hard fluorescent light hit us.

"What in the world!" Mrs. Newbery was standing there with her hands on her hips. "I didn't see you two at first. Have you been in this room all along?"

"Yep," Aaron said, lightning-quick.

"Well, cut along home," Mrs. Newbery said, "and let me lock up. And shut down the computers."

I was ready to pull their plugs permanently.

We filed out. My head felt like a melon. You can get jet lag from this kind of behavior. We were walking out over the crummy tile floors of the Vanderwhitney part of school. Outside, raw winter weather hit us. There was some snow in the air, and the last buses had gone. We turned toward Fifth Avenue, trudging, silent.

"Anyway, now we know who extinguished the blaze before the hook and ladder company got there," Aaron said.

"Us," I said, totally psyched.

"How you got to go along, Josh, I can't figure at all," he said. "You were standing too close or something."

"Aaron, please," I said. "I've got a headache the size of Lincoln Center."

"No pain, no gain," he said. "Josh, we both did it. We cellular-reorganized back like seventy-five years.

We're not talking information superhighway here. We're talking a toll-free ten-lane expressway. And we're on it—in both directions. Talk about interactive."

I let him rattle on. What choice did I have? He tried to walk out into traffic at the Eighty-sixth Street intersection. Part of me was still back in the Vanderwhitneys' library all those thousands and thousands of afternoons ago. I thought I could smell smoke in my dress code, under the Bulls warm-up jacket.

"Kids." Aaron shook his head. "If that was Cuthbert's idea of playing, thank heaven for *Wolfenstein* and *Sim City 2000.* When you get right down to it, there's nothing safer and more user-friendly than a video game."

But I couldn't get my mind away from where we'd been. "If we hadn't put out that fire, the room would have gone up like a torch. Curtains, rugs, polish on everything—that room was totally . . ."

"Combustible," Aaron said.

The whole idea that we saved Cuthbert and Lysander Vanderwhitney's lives, especially Lysander's, all those years before we were even born was still a hard concept for me. Now Aaron was quiet.

"There's more to this process than I thought," he said after a while.

"Meaning?"

"Well, I've made three trips, right? The first time I saw Heather practically wiped out on a horse in traffic. The second time, when I went backward, I saw that girl and that guy doing all that worried kissing. They were like really furtive. This time it was a kid trying to barbecue his brother. Think about it."

"Like they're all connected?"

"I'm afraid so. I never seem to run into anybody just reading a book or taking a nap. People sleep a third of the time, you know."

"I know. So?"

"It looks like my formula depends on Emotional Component at the other end."

"You mean—"

"Right. Every time I get there, somebody's upset about something. Turning up just in time for trouble could be a problem. I've got mega-diddling to do."

We continued trudging home. When I got off the elevator on twelve, Aaron's lips were moving, but his mind was somewhere else.

Even though I'd taken a really long way home, Mom wasn't there yet. Without an O Pear, Heather and I were turning into a couple of latchkey kids. The apartment was all shadowy. But when I went into my room, all the lights were on.

A girl was sitting on my bed. She was in dress code: white blouse with collar, Pence plaid skirt. But she wasn't Heather. She was sitting on my bed in big shoes, legs crossed, making herself at home and talking on my phone.

When she saw me, her pale eyebrows jumped up high on her pale forehead. She slapped her hand over the phone. "Who do you think you are?"

"I think I'm Josh. I think this is my room."

"Josh who?"

"I live here."

"You're like Heather's brother?" Boy, was she annoyed.

I nodded.

"Heather never mentioned she had a brother."

"Figures," I said. "Who are you?" But I had a pretty good idea.

Her eyebrows shot up even higher. "Camilla Van Allen, of course. Just shut up a minute. I'm on the phone."

Then she went back to her conversation. "Oh, Junior," she said in a whole new voice, "I'm sorry. I was interrupted by some little creep in a Huckley tie. Heather's brother or somebody. I'd love to come to the party Friday night. Heather too. We'd bring her cousin, Feona Foxworthy, but Feona had to fly back to England for a point-to-point. What? Of course we can come. What do you think we are, seventh graders?"

It went on like that. Finally Camilla signed off.

"But you are seventh graders," I said.

"In our case it doesn't count," Camilla said. "Heather's emotionally fourteen, and I'm a Van Allen. That was Junior Saltonstall. He's having a party at his place Friday night, late. His parents are in the Caribbean. It'll be wall-to-wall upper-school boys. Junior goes to boarding school."

"Then what's he doing home?"

"He was expelled. Isn't it thrilling?"

But then Camilla realized she was talking to somebody's little brother. She stood up, straightened her Pence plaid pleats, propped her hair behind her ears, and headed for my door.

"Heather's in her room on her phone. We have high-profile plans to make about Friday night." Camilla gave me a hard look from the door. "Forget everything you've heard here. If Heather misses this party, I'll hold you responsible." She sucked in her cheeks. "I have influence, Jake."

"Josh," I said.

"You say," she said, and left.

I get hardly any privacy.

I dreamed that night, big time and nonstop. I was falling, of course, plastered to my mattress and falling through time and space. Then I was walking along a street with antique cobblestones. Aaron was there in a Huckley tie. At least this time we had clothes on. It was an eerie street. Everybody was in black—black horses with black feathers on their heads pulling black buggies, funeral wreaths on doors. It was this city of death.

Next to me the dream Aaron said, "Every time I get there, somebody's upset about something. Turning up just in time for trouble could be a problem."

We went around a dark corner. In the distance was the half-finished dome of the U.S. Capitol against a black sky. So this must be Washington, D.C. "I make it the mid-1860's," Aaron said.

"Right," said a man in a beard and a big hat, brushing past us. I think it was Mr. Thaw, our old history teacher.

A large, tear-stained lady in a black bonnet and hoop skirt ran up to us. "Where have you two been?" she shrieked, reaching out and giving Aaron and me a couple of shakes. "You could have saved him!"

"Oh, great," Aaron said hopelessly. "It's Mrs. Lincoln."

I woke up in a sweat, tireder than when I went to bed, and still jet-lagged. But it was a school day.

13

Possible Breakthrough

Aaron was signed out of his morning classes. He was nowhere around at lunch and late for History. You don't sign out of History because the teacher is Mr. L. T. Thaw.

When Aaron came in, I almost didn't know him. His eyes were all baggy, and his red hair was standing up in uncombed clumps. He looked a lot worse than usual.

"Late, Zimmer," Mr. Thaw said. "In this class, that's a—"

"I know." Aaron stood slumped in the doorway. "A misdemeanor." He was fighting a yawn.

"And what progress have you to report on your historical presentation for Parents' Night? Next Tuesday is practically upon us."

"A certain amount," Aaron mumbled. "For one

thing, there was a fire in the Vanderwhitney House part of school. Quite a while back."

Mr. Thaw stared hard at Aaron over the heads of the class. He pulled on his beard. For once everybody was listening.

"Not a major conflagration, I take it?" Mr. Thaw said carefully. He bored holes in Aaron through rimless glasses.

"Not too major," Aaron said.

"Then I don't suppose that event will be of . . . consuming interest to the parents, do you?"

Aaron shrugged. He trudged past my desk on the way to his. Class went on as usual. But his mind sure wasn't on the administration of U. S. Grant.

When the bell finally rang, he veered past me and said, "Meet me at the Black Hole right after school. We're talking possible breakthrough."

I strolled past Mrs. Newbery's desk after school. When I got to the Black Hole door, there was a sign on it:

BOTH COMPUTERS DOWN

The door was open a crack. Aaron's baggy eye peered through at me. He opened the door, yanked me inside, and closed it.

He was really excited and worn out. Not a good combination. "Possible breakthrough. I've got some figures together that might send me where I want to go when I want—"

"Aaron, I don't want to hear about it. I'm trying

to block everything that happened yesterday. For one thing, it gave me a really bad dream."

"It wasn't about the Great Chicago Fire of 1871, was it?"

"No."

"Mine was," he said, "though I didn't get that much sleep. I was up all night, did—"

"Aaron, spare me. Anyway, the computers are down. It says so on the sign."

"No, they aren't. I put up that sign. A fifth grader came in here at lunch to play *Civilization* or something. We don't want to be interrupted."

He was really beginning to treat the Black Hole like his own personal property.

"I've done serious editing on my formula," he said, taking me by the arm. "Now I need you to—"

"Wrong, Aaron," I said. "I'm staying away from those terminals. They could be hazardous to my health. How much reorganization do you think my cells are going to put up with?"

"I'm probably not going anywhere," he said. "I'm only fine-tuning. I want you here just as backup. I don't want you in my force field."

"Just how big is your force field anyway, Aaron?" I said. "You don't know."

"Just stand here by the door. If I happen to be gone for a while, and Mrs. Newbery—"

"I know, I know." I decided I'd better stay and let him play Mad Computer Nerd one more time. "But this is it for me, Aaron. I'm not coming in here anymore.

I'm going to do something else with my life. I'm going to . . . join the chess club or something."

But he was already over between the two glowing screens. His hands were splaying out over the keyboards. I positioned myself against the door with one hand behind me on the knob.

He entered five or six digits. Then it happened. Both screens lit up like Las Vegas. Full-color supergraphics surged. All the air in the Black Hole was charged. I smelled everything—smoke, flowers, furniture polish. My hand gripped the doorknob. I blinked.

When I looked again, Aaron was still there. But somebody else was in the room, standing between us. One second she wasn't there. The next she was.

It was a girl, older than we were, almost a grown-up. I wasn't sure. Whatever she was wearing, a costume or a uniform, made her look older. She had something in her hand: a feather duster. She seemed to be trying to dust the back of Aaron's head. Then she dropped the feather duster, clutched her head, and screamed.

"Don't!" I said, plastering myself against the door. "This is a boys' school!"

14

The Past People

Aaron whirled around. He was almost standing on her feet. She wore high-heeled lace-up shoes with toes that came to points. Her dress was as black as last night's dream. Both her hands clutched her cheeks. She was really quivering.

"Back to the drawing board," Aaron said quietly.

"Who do you think you are?" she said to us, finding her voice.

"Aaron, who do you think she is?" I said.

He knew. He pointed a small finger at her. "You'd be the girl kissing that guy. You'd been crying," he said in a spooky voice. "You wear a ring on a little chain around your neck inside your dress."

Her hands drew down her face. She was pretty. "Attend to your own business," she said very strict. "And what have you done with the library? What Mrs. Vanderwhitney will say about this, I shouldn't like to think, I'm sure."

She was English. You could hear it in her voice. And really upset. Talk about Emotional Component.

"I was running a feather duster over the library table. It isn't my responsibility. But the other servants are American, so you don't get a full day's work out of them."

"Were you like upset about something at the time?" Aaron asked carefully. "Like emotional?"

There were tears in her lashes. But then her cells had just been reorganized, and that hurts.

She shot him a look. "Servants are not expected to have emotions," she said. "I was merely going about my business, dusting the library table. Then suddenly it was replaced by these objects."

She pointed to the glowing computer screens. She looked down. "And what have you done with the floors?" She turned to the blank wall. "The window! Where is it? And we had just replaced the curtains with best Brussels lace."

She wrung her hands. She really was pretty, and very neat. Her dark hair was smoothed back and parted in the center. "And who are you two?"

"I'm Josh," I said. "This is Aaron. Everything's his fault."

"Am I being held for ransom?" Her chin went up. "You might better have abducted Cuthbert. Indeed, you're welcome to him."

Aaron put up a hand. "Let me explain," he said, though there was something hopeless in his voice. He kicked off by telling her what year it is.

Her eyes got big. They were a nice shade of blue and now huge.

"The Vanderwhitneys don't . . . live here anymore," Aaron told her. "They probably sold their house to the school. The school's called Huckley."

"Huckley?" the girl said. "Poppycock. The Huckleys live two doors along, just before the Havemeyers."

"Havemeyer House is where we have lunch," I said.

"And what of the Van Allens next door?" she said, softer. Her hand came up and touched the gold chain inside her collar.

"Van Allen House is part of the school too. It's mostly classrooms."

She stood quiet, thinking hard. She glanced past Aaron at the terminals. "And those devices?"

"That's a little harder to explain," Aaron said. "We're into artificial intelligence here and chronological flow charts. We're—"

"Are they time machines?" she said.

We stared.

"Basically," Aaron said. "In layman's terms."

"I've read Mr. H. G. Wells," she said. "I am an educated girl, you know. I am not a common servant. I was brought to this country as governess to Cuthbert and Lysander. Of course they aren't ready for a governess. I was forced to be nursery maid, even to that great lump of an overgrown boy, Cuthbert."

Aaron nodded. "You're overeducated and underemployed in a prefeminist time frame."

She gave us both a look as stern as Mr. L. T. Thaw's. I thought Aaron and I were too old to be governessed, but she was a take-charge type of girl.

"The pair of you have been in my—time. You were there the day of the fire, weren't you? I knew someone had been in the room. I caught a glimpse of you. Cuthbert took credit for putting out the flames. But no one would take Cuthbert for a hero."

"We were there," Aaron admitted.

"Then you may send me straight back, and we'll say no more about it," she said. "And look sharp. I haven't got all day. If I go missing, Mrs. Vanderwhitney will dock my pay. She is a well-known skinflint. And I have . . . personal matters to attend to."

She was geared up to go. She smoothed down her hair and straightened her uniform skirt. She reached down for her feather duster. "Where do you want me?"

Aaron looked as worried as I'd ever seen him. He didn't look like he even knew how he'd gotten her here. He sure didn't know how to get her back.

"When Josh and I were in your time," he said, stalling, "we just came back when our . . . time was up."

"Well, I shan't wait for that, if you don't mind," she said very brisk.

"Okay," he mumbled. "I'll give it a shot, but it's a needle in a haystack. You can stand right there. I guess."

When he turned to the keyboards, he looked

shrunken and unsure. His hands splayed out, but came back. He tried again. I was hanging on the doorknob, afraid to blink. He entered digits. He zeroized and tried some more.

No power surge. Nothing. The figures glowed dim on the screens. He pushed the Escape button, but nobody did. Time passed. But it was just regular, now-type time. I could read Aaron's mind through the back of his head. His own personal memory bank was a dead letter box.

He turned around. "I'll use my original formula, prediddled," he said, trying to sound certain. "I'll try to go back and take you with me," he told the girl. "Stand right behind me and put both your hands on my shoulders."

She propped her feather duster under her arm and dropped her hands on his bony shoulders. His hands went out. Digits unfurled. The room lurched. I hung on the knob. But the formula misfired. We were all still there.

Over Aaron's shoulders I could read the word pulsing on both screens:

ERROR ERROR

He turned and put up his hands. "This could take some time," he said without a glimmer of hope. "A few days . . . a few nights . . ."

"How very inconvenient," the girl said.

"I can't help it," said the A-to-Z man. "I'm only eleven."

I moaned.

"Aaron, you better come up with the formula of your life. Maybe she isn't ever going to go back on her own. Maybe what worked for us doesn't work for . . . the past people. Maybe she isn't bidirectional."

"I'll get her back," he said in his mouse voice.

"You say," I said. "And what do we do with her in the meantime? Hide her in here, bring her food, and put papers down? She isn't a puppy."

"Kindly don't speak of me as if I weren't here," the girl said. "I am."

"The janitor comes in here at night and sort of sweeps around. He'll find her. He'll throw her out. She'll be homeless. It's winter. She doesn't have a warm coat."

"Josh, do I have to think of everything?" Aaron whined. "It's your turn. Use your initiative."

When my brain goes on overload, I think in every direction. My head throbbed. *I am not a common servant*, the girl had said. That rang a bell. And I was desperate.

"I don't believe I caught your name," I said, trying for polite.

"Phoebe," she said.

Phoebe? First, Fenella. Next, Feona. Then . . .

"Phoebe," I said, "are you familiar with the term 'O Pear'?"

15

Cabbages and Kings

We pulled up three chairs, and I tried to put Phoebe in the picture. I started with what O Pears are.

"They're English girls from very nice backgrounds," I said. "They come over here to help out with families and to see American life. They're here to expand their horizons, and ours."

"But don't they take jobs away from governesses and nannies and nursery maids?" Phoebe looked concerned.

"We don't have too many governesses and nannies and nursery maids anymore," I said. "Now it's mostly baby-sitters, the occasional Mr. Mom, day care, and *Sesame Street*."

Phoebe had pulled a lace handkerchief out of her sleeve and sat there twisting it in both hands.

"My dad's in Chicago, and my mom works," I said,

starting to explain my family and easing up to Heather. "Heather's going to sneak out to a party Friday night. But don't worry about her. She comes. She goes." The explanation took me a while. Finally Aaron tapped his watch. It was quarter till five. It was time to leave if we were going.

And Phoebe was still with us.

"You want to give it one more try?" Aaron's eyes were begging her. "You want to try to—think yourself back? Really put your mind to it."

She closed her eyes and gripped her handkerchief. But Emotional Component didn't seem to do her any good. Maybe in her heart she wasn't that anxious to get back to Cuthbert and Lysander.

"Okay," Aaron said finally. "Let's take her to your place, Josh. It'll just be . . . temporary. I'll be doing some heavy-duty collating and really taking a hard look at my formula. You'll be back to 1923 in no time, Phoebe. One way or another. Until then, you can just O Pear at Josh's house. It'll be—cool."

Easy for him to say.

"What choice have I?" Phoebe reached for her feather duster. "I trust I can be a useful servant in any household."

"Don't think of yourself as a servant," I told her. "Think of yourself as a helpful guest."

We cracked the door and peered out at the empty media center. Mrs. Newbery was long gone. Some nights she locks up. Some nights she just gives up. Down the dark hall through Van Allen House we moved like shadows. But I knew Phoebe was real. You could hear the sharp sound of her high heels on the crummy tile.

The front door of Huckley House was in sight when a figure loomed out of a classroom. We pulled back into a stairwell. It was Mr. Thaw, always the last teacher to leave. He swept out ahead of us with his tweed coat flapping behind him.

"That's our old history teacher," I told Phoebe. "He's making us do a report for Parents' Night next Tuesday." I thought I'd just fill her in as we went along.

Outside, a sleety wind was blowing. Phoebe didn't have a coat, so Aaron and I pooled our money to see if we had enough for a cab. We did. Aaron nodded at the drugstore on the Madison Avenue corner. "We better drop in there first, then catch a cab. Phoebe will need a toothbrush."

Aaron was okay on details, but he was sure leaving the big picture to me. When we got out of the cab at our building, he handed over three dollars and a dollar tip.

"Outrageous," Phoebe said. "Highway robbery. That was a fifty-cent trip and a dime tip. It wasn't even a proper cab. And certainly not a proper driver. He didn't even get out to open the door for us. What has the world come to?"

I had a bad feeling that Phoebe was in for worse shocks than that. Heather, for one.

When the elevator got to twelve, Aaron stayed on for the penthouse. He said his job was to collate, diddle, and fiddle all night. I jammed the elevator door open with a foot. "Aaron, you're leaving me with the hard part. If I'm going to turn Phoebe into an O Pear, I'll have to tell a lot of lies to my mom, because she certainly isn't going to buy the truth. I'm going to have to convince Heather. I'm in deep—"

"You'll be fine," he said, but his mind was already upstairs at his workstation. His foot nudged mine out of the door, and it closed between us.

Nobody was home yet. Camilla Van Allen wasn't even on my phone. I showed Phoebe around, pointing out Dad's den where she'd sleep. She observed everything and checked a flat surface for dust. In the kitchen I talked her through the electric can opener and the microwave.

"Have you a cook?" she asked.

"Just us, when we get around to it. We mainly defrost things." I showed her the freezer compartment at the top of the refrigerator.

"Upstairs maid?" Phoebe's eyebrows could get kind of high on her forehead, like Camilla's.

"We don't have an upstairs," I said.

"Butler?"

"We only have a doorman, Vince. But he's downstairs. He doesn't—buttle."

"Who cleans your grates?"

"What are they?"

"The hearths. Fireplaces."

"We don't have any. We have central heat, central air."

"How very sad," Phoebe said, "not to have a cheery fire to sit before in the evenings and let your mind drift."

"We have TV for that," I said. We were in the living room, and I was trying to explain TV when the front door banged open. Heather. I know her bang.

She appeared in the living room doorway on the way to her phone. She'd been shopping since school was out. She had three or four Bloomingdale's bags.

"Is Mom home yet?" she said. "Because I've got to get these things I'm wearing to Junior Saltonstall's party hidden before she—"

Heather caught her first glimpse of Phoebe. Phoebe folded her hands in front of her and lined up the points of her lace-up shoes. She had excellent posture.

Heather blinked.

I was beginning to get used to Phoebe, but she came as a surprise to Heather. Heather stared, starting with Phoebe's feet. She seemed to approve of the shoes, which were retro-funky now. She wondered about the white stockings. I guess they were stockings. They probably wouldn't be panty hose. Heather's stare hung around Phoebe's waistline for a while. She nodded cautiously at the starchy lace collar—more retro. Phoebe's face was pretty, so doubt filled Heather's. She ended up at Phoebe's smooth hair pulled back in a knot behind.

"Who—"

The front door opened behind Heather, and she jumped. Mom.

"Heather," Mom sighed behind her. "Is my Bloomingdale's charge card anywhere on your person?"

"Look," Heather said, pointing toward the living room.

Mom came in in her Adidas, unwinding a long scarf from around her neck. Her nose was nipped red because she'd walked home from Barnes Ogleby. She saw Phoebe. Sometimes I can read Mom's mind. This time it was blank.

"Mom," I said in a funny, high voice, "this is Phoebe. Au Pair Exchange sent her. They called up, and they—said she was coming. She might be a little jet-lagged. Au Pair Exchange said they were really sorry that Fenella and Feona didn't work out. So they sent Phoebe. She's like a—bonus. British Air lost her luggage. All she's got is a toothbrush."

Phoebe had parked her feather duster in the front hall. "And a feather duster." I'd been on a roll. Now I began to run down.

Mom gazed at both of us. She was really dubious.

"Phoebe," I said in a screechy soprano like Lysander's, "this is my mom, Mrs. Lewis. This is my sister, Heather."

"Good evening, madam," Phoebe said. "Good evening, miss."

Heather gawked. Mom couldn't take her eyes off Phoebe's hands cupped together in front of her waist.

"You're English?" Mom said.

"I am indeed, madam," Phoebe said. "A loyal subject of His Majesty, good King George the Fifth."

Mom wondered. Heather swayed. Phoebe was such a jump from Fenella and Feona, Heather didn't know what to think.

"We've had our difficulties with Au Pair Exchange," Mom said.

"I hope I shall give satisfaction, madam." Phoebe's eyes skated down to Mom's running shoes, which she didn't understand. "I have most recently been in the employ of Mrs. Van—"

"Phoebe's O Peared a lot, Mom. Au Pair Exchange is sending a printout all about her. It's in the mail. She's seventeen and a recent . . . school leaver."

"Thank you for sharing, Josh," Mom said. Her mind was a mixture of suspicion and surprise.

"We hope you'll—make yourself at home, Phoebe," she said. "I don't know what we have for dinner. I could defrost—"

"I shall see to it, madam, as you are rather short of staff at the moment." Hands still cupped, Phoebe walked poker-straight out of the living room, heading for the kitchen.

The three of us looked at each other. My face was blank.

"At least you won't be going to any discos on horseback with this one," Mom said to Heather. "And Josh, you either know more about Phoebe than you're telling, or less. When you can come up with a good explanation for your part in this, I'll be glad to hear it."

I was in my room when my phone rang. For once it was for me.

Aaron. "Is Phoebe still there?"

"She's here," I said. "And get to work. If she—vanishes, I'll let you know. Don't be calling every five minutes."

After a long time a strange smell began to seep in under my door. I couldn't place it. It wasn't anything burning. It was worse than that.

I went out into the hall. Mom and Heather were already there. "Gross me out," Heather said. "What *is* that?"

"Cabbage," Mom said. "I'd bought a head of cabbage for coleslaw. Phoebe's boiling it."

"I'll order a pizza and have it in my room," Heather said. "I've got a conference call coming in from Camilla anyway."

"You'll be at the dinner table with the rest of us, young lady," Mom said. "If we have to eat it, you have to eat it. Josh, drop by the kitchen and see if you can do anything."

The boiling cabbage smell about knocked me out when I opened the kitchen door. Phoebe had found an apron. "Oh, Josh, did you say this microwave machine will cook anything in minutes?" She wiped her shiny forehead with a floury arm.

"Sure."

"Then would you fire it up?"

I opened the microwave door. A dish was inside with mashed potatoes on top. It didn't look too bad. I gave it a few minutes full power.

"Shepherd's pie," Phoebe said, "made from bits and bobs I discovered in the icebox."

"Refrigerator," I said.

"I'm a dab hand with pastry," she said, whatever that meant. "I'll do a proper job of baking tomorrow. If I am still here. I'll do you a nice jam roly-poly for pudding."

"Sounds . . . great," I said. But the boiling cabbage smell was really cutting my eyes. "About the cabbage—"

"An excellent winter vegetable," she said. "I knew you'd like it." She was still somewhat stunned by being here, but her training was taking over. She leaned nearer me. "Aaron seems to think I might go back suddenly, all on my own."

"He hopes," I said.

"But supposing I did? Wouldn't your mother think it odd if I suddenly vanished?"

"Don't worry about that," I said. "The other O Pears vanished pretty quick too. But there could be another problem—about you being a loyal subject of good King George Whatever."

Phoebe listened.

"Heather wouldn't have picked up on it, but Mom wondered. You English people have a queen now. Good Queen Elizabeth the Second."

Phoebe's eyes widened. "You mean . . . the king—"

"I'm afraid that king's been gone quite a while. Aaron would know when."

Phoebe's blue eyes filled.

"Phoebe, you've got to remember. Things change."

The microwave bell rang. She stood up ramrod stiff

and blinked away her tears. Mom was there in the kitchen door behind me.

"Dinner is served, madam," Phoebe said.

When I woke up the next morning, hints of last night's cabbage were still hanging around. But the smell of frying bacon was seeping in too. Which might also mean eggs. On my bedside table was a steaming cup of tea with milk already added. So Phoebe was still with us.

Mom and Heather were out in the hall with cups of tea in their hands.

"Some service," Mom said. She was still in her robe, but she had her face on.

"Wait till Camilla hears," Heather said. "The Van Allens have a whole staff of servants, of course."

"Don't think of Phoebe as a servant," Mom said. But her heart wasn't in it.

16

A Question of Time

Aaron and I took the bus that Friday morning. "Is Phoebe—"

"She's still here," I told him. "You up all night?"

"Most of it," he said. "How are things at your place?"

"Not too bad. Mom's suspicious."

"Moms are," Aaron said.

"Who was the King of England in Phoebe's time?"

"George the Fifth," Aaron said.

"That's him. He's dead, right?"

"1936."

"I figured. Phoebe was upset about that. And she's not too pleased about sitting at the table with us for meals. She says it isn't proper. But cabbage tastes better than it smells. A little. Phoebe cooks. For tonight she's fixing toad-in-the-hole."

Aaron looked up. "Actual toad?"

"That's what we were afraid of. But toad-in-the-hole is just an English term for sausages in a batter, microwaved. We're having jam roly-poly for dessert."

"Sounds like a month's worth of calories," Aaron the herbivore said. "But hang in there. I'll sign out of my morning classes. Mr. Headbloom will cover for me. By noon I might have some solid progress to report."

As soon as we got to school, Aaron headed toward the media center. "Come on," he said. "We've got some time before homeroom."

"Aaron, read my lips. I told you I wasn't going near the Black Hole again."

"You want Phoebe to get back?" he said. "Your mom's going to figure out Au Pair Exchange didn't send her. It's just a question of time. And the Vanderwhitneys are going to wonder where she is. She could lose her job at that end, you know. Besides, I've got a lot on my mind and too many digits in my head. We're in this together, Josh."

"Aaron, you don't even remember those digits you entered when Phoebe suddenly turned up. You were winging it, right?"

"I'm closing in on a breakthrough," he said, not answering. "I'm on the brink of finding a bidirectional fiber. I'm on the threshold of pinpointing a foolproof three-dimensional fax. You've heard of multicultural? I'm about to be multichronological. I'm—"

"Aaron, your problem is you can get us into trouble, but you can't get us out."

We were strolling past Mrs. Newbery's desk. She was

already at it. "Just a moment, Aaron," she said. We froze.

She handed over a Xeroxed sheet. "This is the last reference to the Vanderwhitney family I can find for you in the 1920's *New York Times Index*," she said, "except for an obituary, which is a real downer."

"Appreciate it, Mrs. Newbery," Aaron said, cool as a cucumber. "This will be a big help for our Parents' Night report next week." We strolled on toward the Black Hole, taking our time. The BOTH COMPUTERS DOWN sign was still on it.

Inside, we looked over the sheet. You could see the date on this one—November 1929:

Palatial Home of Late Osgood Vanderwhitney to Serve as Wing of New Huckley School

> The Huckley School that has already acquired the properties of the Havemeyer, Huckley, and Van Allen families is proposing to purchase the home of Osgood Vanderwhitney from his estate.
>
> The house, called the most tasteful built in the city during 1921, has recently been the residence of Osgood Vanderwhitney and his son Cuthbert, aged fifteen and now at boarding school. Osgood Vanderwhitney's tragic death has shaken the social and financial communities. See obituary for details of his leap from the window of his Wall Street office following the recent Market Crash.

"What's all this?" I said.

"Osgood Vanderwhitney took a dive," Aaron said.

"I see that. But why had he been living in this house with just Cuthbert? That would make anybody jump out a window. What happened to Mrs. Vanderwhitney? What about Lysander? You don't suppose Cuthbert . . ."

The Black Hole was dead silent. We glanced around.

"Maybe little Lysander vanished without a trace," Aaron said in a spooky voice.

"Phoebe—"

"Phoebe wouldn't know yet. It would have happened after she . . . came here." Aaron gazed down at the floor like there could be a small body buried there. Bones now.

"A rich kid disappearing would have made *The New York Times*," I pointed out.

"Not necessarily." Aaron's imagination was really on the move now. "The Vanderwhitneys might have covered up the crime to save Cuthbert and their reputation. They could have said Lysander went off to boarding school. Why not? He was probably way smarter than Cuthbert."

"Knock it off, Aaron." When you get right down to it, he's really safer working at the computers than when his mind starts wandering. The bell for homeroom went, and so did I.

"Skip lunch and be here," Aaron said.

At noon I swung by the Havemeyer House lunchroom and bought us a couple of tuna salads on pita bread and some Snapple.

When I passed through the BOTH COMPUTERS DOWN door, Aaron was hard at work. "I'm practically there.

I've got a lock on that time Phoebe came from. My technology is really beginning to catch up with concept."

I gave him a tuna pita, but he didn't have time for it. "Look, yesterday I entered these digits, combined them with a graphic, and—"

"You zeroized."

"That didn't get me anywhere. If I change that last digit to this—"

It was like the room imploded. Fire flashed. Both computers wobbled. Snapple went everywhere. I grabbed for Aaron, but he stayed where he was. All his red hair was standing up. Air seeped back into the room.

But we weren't alone.

"You two again," a high voice barked. "Who do you think you are?"

Aaron and I spun around.

Cuthbert Vanderwhitney was standing there. We'd only seen him with his feather headdress. His hair was cut in a Dutch boy style. His pudgy fists were on his knickered hips. His freckles glowed in full color, and his lower lip was out a mile.

Aaron's head dropped on his chest.

"What have you done with Lysander?" I said, because Aaron had me totally psyched.

Cuthbert scowled. "I beat him up regularly. It keeps him in line."

"But—"

But it wasn't near 1929 yet. Cuthbert looked the

same as the last time we saw him. He'd still be about fourth grade, though he was as big as me, bigger than Aaron.

His eyes crackled. His feet in high-top shoes were planted wide. He wore long argyle socks, corduroy knickers, and a weird velvet-looking jacket with gold buttons and a big white collar. A wide tie circled his bulging neck.

"You're trespassing. And it's not your first offense. My papa will have you thrown out." He noticed Aaron's tuna pita. He grabbed it up and smelled it. "I don't eat this," he said, and threw it against the wall.

The pita stuck where it hit. The wall hadn't been there in his time. Cuthbert stared. "What have you done with my house? We're Vanderwhitneys, you know."

Aaron was recovering. "Let me put it in a nutshell for you, Cuthbert," he said. "You've cellular-reorganized three-quarters of a century ahead of your time. Your family's house is a school now."

Cuthbert trained mean, beady eyes on Aaron. "Liar, liar, pants on fire," he said.

Which was probably his favorite saying.

"It's true," Aaron said. "Believe it." With Cuthbert you have to be firm.

"Aaron, for pete's sake," I muttered, "send him back."

"If it's a school," Cuthbert said, working this out, "who's in charge?"

"You mean like the headmaster?" I said.

"Buster Brewster," Aaron said, and he had a point.

"Harrison K. 'Blackjack' Brewster from Ninety-second Street?" Cuthbert's eyes narrowed.

"No, Buster's probably his grandson or something. Maybe a great-great nephew. Who knows?" Aaron said. "Just stand right there, Cuthbert."

Aaron turned to the computers and started entering digits. Four, five . . . I was braced. But I looked around at Cuthbert because I really wanted to see him dissolve.

He was already gone.

"Aaron."

He looked around. "Hey, I didn't even—"

The Black Hole door was open. Cuthbert had walked out. He was at large in Huckley School. The bell rang, so lunch was over, and it was time for History. You can't sign out of that because Mr. Thaw's the teacher.

Aaron and I ran into each other. Then we ran out the door. We streaked past Mrs. Newbery, but so had Cuthbert. The hallway outside was full of middle-school guys in Huckley dress code.

"It won't be hard to spot him," Aaron said. "He's dressed like Little Lord Fauntleroy."

"And what if we don't?" I said. "He was trouble enough in his own time."

"We'll get him," Aaron said, looking everywhere.

"Before History?" I said. "Because I don't think so."

Aaron skidded to a stop at the door of Mr. L. T. Thaw's classroom. "It's hopeless with all the halls full of people."

"What if some teacher finds him before we do?" I said. "Some adult. Then what?"

"Look," Aaron said, "do you feel like cutting History?"

"No way," I said. We slid into our seats a second before the bell rang.

"Ah, Zimmer," Mr. Thaw said from the front of the room. "An unexpected pleasure to see you here on time." We were up to James A. Garfield, twentieth president of the United States, assassinated in 1881.

The time dragged worse than usual. I tried to pretend that Cuthbert was a bad dream. What Aaron was thinking was anybody's guess. Fifteen minutes, twenty, we were almost halfway through the period.

The door opened. Mr. Thaw looked at it and froze. You'd think he was seeing President Garfield being shot right out there in the hall.

Cuthbert strolled in.

His hands were on his hips. His necktie was tied in a large bow, and there were gold buttons down his front.

Everybody stared because he looked like an exhibit from the Museum of the City of New York. They thought Cuthbert might be curriculum.

"Awright," he said in his piping roar, "keep your seats. Is Buster Brewster in here?"

Mr. Thaw swayed.

"Who wants him?" Buster reared up out of his desk in the middle row.

Buster got a good look at Cuthbert right down to his knickers. The Dutch boy hair. The white collar. The big perky bow tie. The velvet jacket.

"What a wuss," Buster said.

Cuthbert stalked down the aisle. Now he and Buster were nose to nose. Both their necks bulged.

Up at his desk, Mr. Thaw was turning to stone.

Buster couldn't figure out Cuthbert, so he was off guard. "Who do you think you are?" Cuthbert bawled in Buster's big face.

People were getting under their desks. You don't talk to Buster like that. "You're not so tough," Cuthbert bellowed. "And I was here first."

Buster's mighty fists were clenching.

But Cuthbert brought up a powerhouse uppercut and flattened Buster's nose. Cuthbert's left hook had come out of nowhere. Buster went over backward, sprawling across the desk of the kid behind him. Frederick "Fishface" Pierrepont sits behind Buster. But Fishface was already under his desk.

Buster was flat on his back with his legs in the air. Blood was splattered all over his dress code. But he made a comeback. He lunged at Cuthbert. Grabbing for his neck, he got a handful of big white collar instead.

But Buster was off balance before he began. Up came Cuthbert's right fist, also out of nowhere. The sound of knuckles against nose practically echoed. And Buster's face was rearranged one more time.

Buster crumpled.

By then we'd made a big circle around them. Six or eight desks were on their sides. Mr. Thaw unfroze. He's not too steady on his pins anyway. Now he was shaking like a leaf.

Buster was lolling there on Fishface's desk, and you

could see his tongue. Cuthbert with his collar on sideways was reaching for Buster's throat.

"Cuthbert!" Mr. Thaw howled in an ancient voice. "Unhand him at once!"

It was too much for Mr. Thaw. His old knees gave out, and he slumped to the floor. It looked like our history teacher might be—history. He was out cold at least.

The whole room was up for grabs. A boys' school is always about *this close* to a riot anyway. Fists went up all over the room. Quite a few people were beginning to settle old scores. More desks went over. Fishface Pierrepont burrowed out from under his. "I'm calling 911," he piped, and rocketed out of the room.

Aaron rose up. Cuthbert was staring down at Mr. Thaw's sprawled shape. Aaron got Cuthbert under an arm and ran him out of the room and down the hall. Classroom doors were beginning to open all the way to the media center. Inside we got lucky because Mrs. Newbery was at lunch. The three of us raced into the Black Hole and banged the door shut.

The tuna pita was still on the wall. The floor was sticky with Snapple.

"Never laid a finger on me," Cuthbert said. He was blowing on his skinned knuckles. "Those Brewsters always were yellow."

"Aaron," I said, breathing hard. "Send Cuthbert back. Like now. Whatever it takes."

Aaron moved over to the computers, ready to give it a try.

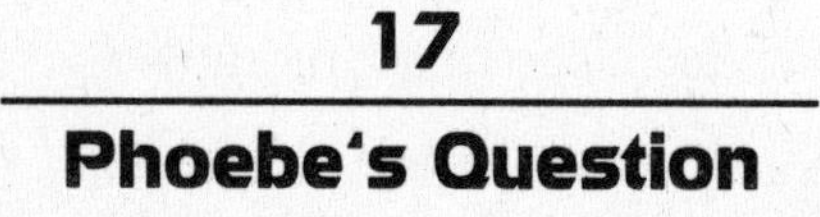

17

Phoebe's Question

Both screens began to fill up with formula. Aaron took his time. Then he was doing some fancy finger work on the keyboard. The screens glowed and pulsed. The ceiling lights dimmed, then surged. One of the fluorescent tubes up there burned out.

But I never took my eyes off Cuthbert. His hands were on his hips, and his high-tops were planted on the floor. Then between one nanosecond and the next, he was nothing but air space. I was looking straight through where he'd been at the tuna pita on the wall.

The room sizzled and fell silent.

"Aaron," I whispered, "you did it."

He turned around to the room with only us in it. He was radish-pale. You never saw so much relief on a human face. He went back to the keyboards.

MISSION

he entered on one screen.

ACCOMPLISHED

he entered on the other.

Then he jumped out of his chair. "YESSSSSS!" he shrieked, and did a complete war dance around the Black Hole without the tomahawk.

"You want to know how I did it?" he said after he'd calmed down a little. "I took my original formula, prediddled, and re-expressed it tomographically."

"Ah," I said.

"You know tomography?"

"No."

"It's diagnostic imaging that directs X rays axially around the human body. In layman's terms."

"Would be."

"Then I got lucky with some random digits. That's what brought both Phoebe and Cuthbert here. To get rid of him, I re-expressed my formula with complements. You know complements?"

"You mean like, 'You look marvelous'?" I said.

"Not that kind of compliment," Aaron said. "A complement is a number representing the negative of a given number. You get it by subtracting each digit of the number from the number representing its base, and in the case of two's complement and ten's, you add unity to the last significant digit. Or in layman's terms, I threw Cuthbert in reverse and sent him on his way."

"Oh," I said. "Or maybe Cuthbert was just ready to go. He'd cleaned Buster's clock. Now he's going back to clean Lysander's."

"Maybe," Aaron said. "But I've got the bugs out, so I can do it again. Bidirectionally. Maybe we can go anywhere in the past we want to, anytime. My formula's still a primitive device. It's covered wagon. But we're looking at Skylab. We're—"

"Have you got enough bugs out of it so people from the past don't keep popping up here? Because I don't think this school can take another dose of Cuthbert."

"I've got some more fiddling to do," Aaron said. "No question about that, but—"

"Aaron," I said. "Let's go home."

He looked around, dazed. His red hair was still on end. His Huckley tie was around under one ear. I wondered if he was too weird to know. "Is school out?" he said.

"Close enough," I said. "The only thing left is math class. I don't think it would do me any good. And I don't think you need it."

He shut down the computers. I peeled the tuna pita off the wall. I hadn't eaten mine either. I dropped them in Mrs. Newbery's wastebasket on our way out. She wasn't back from lunch, but no wonder. School was still in an uproar.

People were milling around out on the sidewalk too. A paramedic van was at the curb to pick up Buster Brewster and Mr. Thaw. Big uniformed guys with rubber gloves were leading Buster into the back of the van. He was holding a bloody towel over his nose. They had Mr. Thaw on a stretcher. He was thrashing around and talking out of his head. So he was alive and kicking, but this looked like his last day of school.

"Now we'll have a sub," Aaron said, "who won't know Warren G. Harding from a hole in the ground."

We walked home.

"Let's go get Phoebe, bring her to school, and send her back to her time," he said. "Mrs. Vanderwhitney will only dock her a day's pay."

That made sense, more or less. "But I wish she'd clear up some things before she goes. Like what happened to Lysander and Mrs. Vanderwhitney. Like why Osgood Vanderwhitney and Cuthbert were living alone in the house by 1929."

"But she won't know," Aaron said. "She's come to us from 1923. That was still all in the future then."

"We could tell her."

"Tell her Osgood Vanderwhitney is going to jump out of a window in Wall Street?" Aaron said. "I don't think so. That would be too creepy for her to know ahead of time. She was upset about King George the Fifth dying, and she didn't even know him."

But she might have an idea about what happened to the Vanderwhitneys. I didn't think little Lysander was buried under the floor of the media center. But you never know.

Aaron was still with me when I slipped the key into our door at home. It opened before I could unlock it.

Phoebe. Mom and Heather had loaned her some clothes, but she was still in her black uniform and starchy collar.

"Great news, Phoebe. Defining moment," Aaron said. "You can—"

"You two young gentlemen had better wash your hands and tidy up a bit. There's cocoa in the kitchen for you afterward."

We filed off and washed.

The kitchen was full of good baking smells. The floor looked like a mirror. "I gave it a good scrub and a coat of wax," Phoebe said. "It was in a shocking state."

Baking, scrubbing, polishing. Even toad-in-the-hole. "I don't think O Pears are supposed to have to do all those things," I told her.

"They sound like useless creatures to me," Phoebe said. "I've run an iron over Miss Heather's new party dress. Clothes are very poor quality these days."

"You've been busy, Phoebe."

"Idle hands are the devil's workshop," she said.

"Are we alone?" I said. "Is Miss—is Heather home yet?"

"She is not," Phoebe said. "And if she is late coming from school, I shall have to speak to madam about it."

"Do that," I said. "And listen to this. We . . . ran into Cuthbert today." Phoebe had been standing over us with her hands cupped. She staggered.

"Right," Aaron said. The mug of cocoa had given him a brown mustache. "My formula went a little haywire and cellular-reorganized Cuthbert. But I think I've got the bugs out of it. We sent him back, and we can send you—"

"Cuthbert?" Phoebe said. "Here?"

"And he isn't all bad," I said. "He beat Buster Brewster to a pulp before he left. But what I want to know is, can you think of anything that might take Mrs. Vanderwhitney and little Lysander . . . away from the family?"

Phoebe's hand crept up to her cheek. She looked away. "It isn't for me to say, I'm sure," she said.

"She suspects something," I said to Aaron. "Even in 1923."

"Kindly don't speak of me as if I weren't here," she said. "As a matter of fact, Mr. and Mrs. Vanderwhitney are not happy in their marriage. They live apart for much of the time."

Phoebe pursed her lips.

"They're going to separate," I said to Aaron.

"Mrs. Vanderwhitney is going to leave Osgood," Aaron said, "and take little Lysander with her. He isn't buried under the floor."

"Certainly not," Phoebe said. "The pair of you gossip worse than servants. But in fact, Mrs. Vanderwhitney has an admirer."

An admirer?

"She is not a bad-looking woman in her way, you know," Phoebe said. "And wealthy in her own right. I fear she's going to run away with a certain gentleman of her acquaintance. Indeed, I've seen a letter or two that has passed between them." Phoebe flushed. "When I was dusting her dressing-table drawers."

"So Mrs. Vanderwhitney is going to take a hike," Aaron said, "and leave Cuthbert behind with Osgood. It fits."

Phoebe nodded sadly. "Yes, I expect any time now that Mrs. Vanderwhitney is going to divorce Mr. Vanderwhitney and marry Mr. Thaw."

Mr. Thaw?

"Mr. Thaw?" Aaron said. Cocoa went everywhere.

"Mr. Thaw?" I said. "You mean she's going to marry our old history teacher?"

Phoebe looked uncertain.

Aaron's head dropped onto the kitchen table. "Josh, you goofball," he said, "her Mr. Thaw would be long gone. Don't you get it?"

"Get what?"

"Mrs. Vanderwhitney married Mr. Thaw. And Mr. Thaw adopted Lysander."

"I still don't get it."

"Josh," Aaron said, "our history teacher, Mr. L. T. Thaw, is Lysander. Lysander Theodore Thaw."

Aaron looked up from the table. We stared at each other.

"Couldn't be," I said.

"Is," Aaron said. "Think about this afternoon. Mr. Thaw yelled out Cuthbert's name."

I remembered that.

"How would he know it?" Aaron said. "And the shock of seeing Cuthbert just the way he'd been way back when Cuthbert was beating him up regularly and trying to barbecue him—it knocked Mr. Thaw out."

My head was pounding, and Phoebe looked puzzled. "Of course he would be a very old man now," she said.

"He is," I said. "He should have retired a long time ago. But he probably thinks he owns the place. He was that old geezer who came out of the classroom last night with his coat flapping. You saw him, Phoebe."

"Little Lysander," she said softly, "after all this time." Her blue eyes had a lot of long distance in them.

"And if he is still here," she said, "am I?"

18

Midnight on the Nose

Phoebe's question hung over the kitchen.

Aaron didn't ask her if she wanted to go back to 1923 this afternoon. She didn't seem that anxious to leave yet. She had things on her mind. And she couldn't stop reaching for the gold chain inside her collar.

The front door banged. You know who.

Heather's head appeared around the kitchen door. "Yo, Pencil-Neck," she said to Aaron, overlooking me. "Listen, Phoebe, I have this friend coming over probably. We have vital plans to make. How about some cucumber sandwiches?" Then she was gone.

Phoebe tinkled a little laugh, the first we'd heard. "Imagine cucumbers in the market at this time of year," she said. "She and her friend will have to settle for hot buttered scones and strawberry jam."

"Actually, cucumbers are in the market this time of year these days," I said. "Everything is."

"How sad," she said. "Is there nothing left to look forward to anymore, not even long summer afternoons and cucumber sandwiches for tea?"

Then Mom appeared in the kitchen in her business suit and Adidas. "What good smells," she said. Her eyes popped. The floor you could see your face in. Everything dusted to death. Phoebe was taking a long pan of scones out of the oven.

"Pinch me," Mom murmured. "This is too good to be true." She saw Aaron and me. We'd finished off the cocoa and were trying to look like a couple of innocent kids.

"I better be getting home," Aaron said.

"Tea, madam," Phoebe said, holding out the pan of scones. "In the drawing room."

I walked Aaron to the elevator. "Listen," he said, "when Phoebe's ready to go back, let me know."

"It's Friday night," I said. "What are we supposed to do, break into school over the weekend? You can't send her back from your home microsystem workstation, can you?"

"Too risky," he said. "Better use two terminals. We can't do much till Monday. But keep me informed."

"Keep yourself informed," I said. "You're always running out on me and leaving me with the hard stuff." The elevator door closed between us.

Heather and Mom and Phoebe were in the living

room with our best teacups. Heather was restless because Camilla hadn't shown. Mom had buttered herself a hot scone. Phoebe was perched on the edge of a chair because Mom had told her to sit down with us. I eased in.

"Phoebe," she said, "these scones absolutely melt in the mouth. You're a real treasure."

"Thank you, madam." Phoebe's hands made a little nest of themselves in her lap.

"But we don't know very much about you," Mom said in a firm voice. "Your family, for instance."

"Oh," Phoebe said, "the Vander—"

"Mom means your own family, Phoebe," I said. "Back home in England."

"I haven't any parents, madam," Phoebe said. "My brother and I are orphans. We grew up in the asylum. Then he emigrated to New Zealand after the Great War."

"Desert Storm," I said. "Right?"

"If you say so," Phoebe murmured. "Of course, all English people have the royal family," she said carefully. "Good Queen Elizabeth the Second." Phoebe beamed. She was proud of herself for that, but I thought we were about one more question from big trouble.

Phoebe thought so too. She stood up. "But I mustn't sit here chatting. I had better see to my toad-in-the-hole." She did her good-posture walk out of the room.

"There's something about that girl I can't quite put my finger on," Mom said. I just sat there, picking some raisins out of my scone. But I could feel Mom's gaze.

"So what?" Heather said. "She makes my bed."

"Well, don't get too used to it, young lady," Mom said. "I have the feeling Phoebe won't be with us for long."

I jumped. Raisins went everywhere.

"Mo-om," Heather said. "You're not going to send her back to England *too*."

"Not on your life." There was a small smile on Mom's face and scone crumbs around her mouth. She was looking into the bottom of her teacup. "But Phoebe's in love."

"Mom," Heather said, "how would you know *that*?"

"I've been in love," Mom said. "I know the signs. It's always a secret you can't keep. And what's that on the chain she wears around her neck? I'll bet it's an engagement ring. Phoebe has a young man. Somewhere."

But Heather was beginning to pace. Camilla hadn't shown. And they had major plans to make about Junior Saltonstall's late-night party. Since it was tonight, Heather was practically down to the wire. She had her dress. But she was going to have to get out of the apartment in the middle of the night. I can read Heather's mind. Basically, it's not that complicated.

We had toad-in-the-hole for dinner and jam roly-poly for dessert. Not a bad meal, but it was like trying to digest a giant hockey puck. We all turned in early, especially Heather. But I was up and down most of the night.

Also, I was monitoring Heather.

At eleven by my digital clock, she was out of bed and

bumping quietly around her room. I had my ear to my door. By eleven-fifteen I was back in bed pretending to be asleep because Heather was heading down the hall and might be planning to use my bathroom. Her bathroom is right next to Mom's room.

Heather cracked my door. This must have been eleven-sixteen. I was breathing steady. She crept across the room to my bathroom. I heard her new dress rustle and smelled Mom's perfume. Heather didn't turn the light on in my bathroom till she'd closed the door.

I slid out of bed and put an ear to the keyhole. Heather was whispering. She'd brought her phone.

"I'm dressed," she said. "I'm like ready to rock. No, I can't talk louder. I'm in Josh's bathroom. Who is he? He's my little brother. I'm wearing heels. Are you wearing heels? How high? I'm wearing blush. Are you wearing . . ."

It went on like that. Then she said, "Okay, but when you get here, knock softly. I'll be waiting by the door. Come in with your shoes off. You can change in my room. We can take a cab from here." Then she signed off.

I had time to get back into bed because she was doing something at my sink and probably looking at herself in my mirror. Then the bathroom door cracked. She was pretty quiet. I'll give her credit for that. I let her get right by my bed.

Then I said, "How's Camilla getting out?"

My voice came out of the dark, so it probably sounded louder than it was. Heather stifled a scream. I flipped on my lamp.

There she stood with her hand clapped over her mouth. Her eyes were huge and all made up. Her hair was practically standing up from shock. But she'd done something funny and new with it anyway. She had on her new party dress. Black, of course. The skirt was so short it reminded me of the Hefty bag she wore downtown to Fenella's club. She was carrying her shoes and her phone.

"If you rat on me, I'll have your guts for garters," she barked in a loud whisper.

I eased up on my pillow. "Hey, I'm sound asleep. But how's Camilla getting out? Just curious."

Heather sighed. "She told her parents she was spending the night with her grandmother who lives around the corner on Seventy-second. Getting out of her grandmother's place is a piece of cake. Her grandmother's real old. She goes to bed early. But she's a light sleeper, so Camilla's going to get dressed here. Josh, if I miss this party, my life's over. It's that simple. So put a sock—"

"I'm fast asleep." I laced my fingers under my chin and closed my eyes. But I was still sitting up and the light was on. Heather crept out of the room.

I turned out the light. Sometimes you can hear better in the dark. Around eleven-thirty I was drifting off when I heard a quiet knock on the front door. Then some rustling. I dozed, but something brought me around. My clock said eleven-fifty. It must have been the front door closing behind Heather and Camilla. They'd be out by the elevator now, putting on their shoes. I drifted off again.

A sharp rap knocked me awake at eleven-fifty-four. Somebody was outside Mom's door.

"Madam," Phoebe said.

I rolled out of bed and cracked my door. Phoebe was still in her uniform. She even had her apron on, tied behind. She was still knocking.

Mom mumbled. She works a full day, so she's tireder at night than Heather.

Phoebe opened Mom's door. The light went on, and I could see a section of Mom trying to sit up. Her hair was in a big tangle.

"Oh, madam, I thought you might require help dressing," Phoebe said.

"I'm dressed," Mom said in a fuzzy voice. "For bed."

"But, madam, I thought you'd be attending the party. Miss Heather has already left." My jaw dropped. Mom bolted up.

"What party?"

"At a Mr. Junior Saltonstall's, I believe," Phoebe said.

Mom was grabbing around for her robe. "Wake up Josh," she said.

I made a run for my bed, dived in, and got the covers up. The room flooded with light. I was breathing steady.

"Josh," Mom said.

I put one eye over the cover and squinted. Mom was standing over me, knotting her robe belt. Phoebe was there, her hands cupped. "But, madam," she said, "I merely assumed you'd be going to the party as well, to chaperone. Surely young girls don't go to parties without their mothers."

She sounded innocent, even a little bewildered. But there was something sly in her eye.

"Josh, what do you know about this?"

"Who, me?"

"Talk to me," Mom said in her firm voice.

"Heather said if I told, she'd have my guts for—"

"I'm listening, Josh," Mom said.

"Junior Saltonstall is having a party at his house, with upper-school guys. Heather has a new dress. She went."

"The Elise and Howard Saltonstalls?" Mom asked.

"I should think so, madam," Phoebe said. "I took the liberty of looking them up in the telephone directory. They are the only Saltonstalls. On Sixty-fifth Street."

"I thought they were in the Caribbean," Mom said.

"They are," I said. "That's why Junior's having a party."

I can read Mom's mind. It was full of drugs, alcohol, and upper-school guys breaking the Saltonstalls' furniture.

"And Heather's out by herself in the middle of the night, heading for that—"

"She's not by herself," I said. "Camilla's with her."

"Camilla?" Phoebe said. She put a hand out on the end of my bed.

"Camilla told her parents she was staying at her grandmother's on Seventy-second. When her grandmother went to sleep, Camilla came over here to change clothes. It was an airtight plan." I checked my clock. "They've only been gone about ten minutes." It was midnight on the nose.

Mom stared away at my ceiling. "This single parenting is a twenty-four-hour-a-day deal," she said. She's thirty-eight, so around then I guess you start talking to yourself.

"All right, Josh," she said. "Get up and get dressed. You and I are going to a party."

"Mom, if Heather finds out I—"

"Up, Josh. We're going to bring Heather home. I want you to see this so-called party for yourself in case you ever think of having one."

Mom stalked out of the room, running hands through her hair.

But Phoebe stayed stone-still at the foot of my bed. "Miss Camilla," she said softly. "Is she a Van Allen?"

I nodded. "And she really lets you know it."

"The Van Allen family live just next door to the Vanderwhitneys, you know. They used to."

"Right," I said. "Now it's all classrooms."

"Mrs. Van Allen, the Mrs. Van Allen of that time, was named Camilla too," Phoebe said, her mind going years back. "But of course that was all long ago, wasn't it?"

And her hand slipped into the collar of her dress.

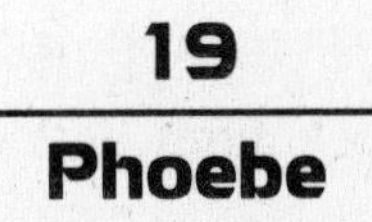

19

Phoebe

Mom was more or less dressed, and I was in my Bulls warm-up jacket. We were zooming down Fifth Avenue in a cab. It was a cold night, but Mom was hot under the collar. She'd actually told the cabby to step on it.

Then we were on our way up in the elevator in the Saltonstalls' building. You could hear the party from here. When the elevator door opened, the party had already spilled out into the hall. Girls and guys all over the place. And enough smoke to pollute your lungs permanently. Everybody had drinks in their hands, and they weren't Snapple.

Some silence fell when Mom and I got off the elevator. I was too young, and she was way too old. She had my hand in a death grip. But I was looking around. After all, this was my first party.

The front door of the Saltonstalls' apartment was open. Inside, it was wall-to-wall preppies and pounding heavy-metal sound. Some people were kind of dancing, but there wasn't a lot of room. When they saw us, they cleared a little path, and Mom kept walking. She had parent written all over her.

"Hey, Junior," somebody said. "Looks like you've got a couple of gate-crashers."

Out of the crowd a guy loomed up, a big sixteen in a damp shirt. He was wearing the official necktie of a well-known boarding school as a belt. And he had a six-pack in each hand. His face was blurred. Junior Saltonstall. "Who do you think—"

Mom shoved him aside.

The living room was a real mob scene. I didn't know you could get that many people into one apartment. The light wasn't too good. The smoke was terrible. Almost everybody was in black, and preppies look a lot alike anyway. The pictures were still on the wall, but the night was young.

Then we saw them. Heather and Camilla were over against a wall, kind of clinging to each other. They were pretty young for this crowd. Their dresses fitted in better than they did. They didn't look like they were having that great a time. I couldn't see how anybody could be having a great time. With the noise and the smell and the crowds, it was like the subway.

"Heather," Mom said.

Heather's made-up eyes enlarged and began to melt. She tried to turn invisible, but her back was to the wall.

"Who *are* those people?" Camilla said. Her pale eyebrows shot up. "Omigosh, it looks like your mother and Jake. Oh, how embarrassing for you, Heather. Couldn't you just die?"

"Mom," Heather said, completely confused. "What am I doing here?"

The next thing I remember, we were in a cab, zooming back uptown. Mom had Heather on one side of her and Camilla on the other. I was practically on the floor.

Heather was getting over the shock and beginning to sulk. Camilla was trying for cool. "Terribly sweet of you to give me a ride home, Mrs. Lewis. But honestly I'll be fine. Grannie knows all about the party. She doesn't expect me back for ages."

"In a pig's eye," Mom said.

We pulled up at Camilla's grandmother's place and got out. She lives in that building on Seventy-second that looks like a cathedral. Tall pointed stained-glass windows and a big, dim lobby with polished wood. The doorman was seven feet tall and had gold braid on his shoulders.

"I am afraid, madam," he said down to Mom, "that Mrs. Van Allen has retired for the evening."

"Wake her up. I'm delivering her granddaughter to her," Mom said brief and firm. "In person."

"Mrs. Van Allen's maid will have retired too, madam," the doorman said. He was also firm. "And she is hard of hearing."

"That's right," Camilla said. "Gladys is as hearing-impaired as a post. She's lots deafer than Grannie. She won't hear a thing. I'll just say good night to you here and—"

"Don't budge, young lady," Mom said to Camilla. "Keep ringing till somebody answers," she told the doorman.

"On your head be it, madam," he said. But he dialed the house phone.

After a lot of rings he was saying, "Mrs. Van Allen, I have a lady in the lobby who wishes to return your granddaughter." He gave us a glance. "No, Camilla is not in her bed. She's in the lobby and dressed for a night on the town."

Camilla propped her hair behind her ears and looked into space.

"Very good, Mrs. Van Allen. I'll instruct them to wait." He hung up. "Mrs. Van Allen will see you in ten minutes exactly. You may take a seat."

It was a long carved bench. Heather wouldn't sit next to me because I'd ratted on her. Mom wouldn't let Heather and Camilla sit together. So it was Heather, then Mom, then Camilla, then me. Heather and Camilla's feet were killing them in those high heels. But nobody spoke. It was one in the morning. I thought being out this late was interesting.

Then the doorman gave us a nod and walked us to the elevator. Camilla was all out of small talk. Heather was still sulking. Her black eyeliner was sliding down her blush. The elevator rose to the Van Allen floor.

Camilla led the way to her grandmother's door, but

she was in no hurry. "I forgot my key," she said in a small voice. But the door was opening anyway.

At first her grandmother was just a dark shape. You could only see her hand. It was real old, just a bunch of bones and veins. An old-fashioned wedding ring and engagement ring were loose on one finger. She was clutching a cane.

The cane came up and aimed at Camilla. "You, young miss," said an ancient voice. "Into your room at once. You will be dealt with later."

Camilla scampered inside, and the apartment swallowed her up. Mrs. Van Allen was still just a dark shape. She saw the three of us out in the hall. Her hand shook. The cane nearly got away from her, but she gripped it.

"Mrs. Lewis?" she said to Mom.

Mrs. Van Allen's gaze swept over us. Her glasses were like nickels winking in the dark. She wore something long and black like a shroud. But it could have been her robe.

"We don't like to disturb you," Mom said, "but I wanted to deliver Camilla to you safe and . . . sound."

"Very kind of you, I'm sure," Mrs. Van Allen said. "But then, you always were." There was the ghost of an English accent in her voice. "Come into the drawing room for a moment. It is so gloomy out here, and I see so dimly now."

She turned around and expected us to follow. Heather hung back, but we did. Mrs. Van Allen needed her cane, but her back was straight. In the dimness her hair glowed white. It was smooth against her old head with a knot behind.

Her drawing room was vast and full of interesting stuff, like the Museum of the City of New York. Marble busts, high-backed furniture, old-time lamps glowing, pictures all over the walls.

She was looking away from us and aiming her cane at the picture of a man over the big stone fireplace. "That is Camilla's late grandfather," she said, "my husband, Gilburtus Van Allen, the handsomest man you ever set eyes on. We defied the world to marry."

She pivoted slowly on her cane. I was standing there. She leaned nearer and examined me. "I married the boy next door," she explained, "and we lived happily ever after."

She looked past me at Mom and Heather. "I won't keep you. But I get so little company these days. Of course, I treasure my privacy. And memories are the best companions. But you must come again soon. To tea. Cucumber sandwiches, I should think, and hot buttered scones with strawberry jam."

They didn't know her. How could they? Her face was all webbed with wrinkles, and her glasses hid her eyes. But I knew who she was. I couldn't believe it. But I knew. She was Phoebe.

20

Parents' Night

It was really late when we got home. Mom was worn out. Heather was still sulking. I was stunned speechless. We all went straight to bed. So it wasn't till the next morning we realized Phoebe was gone.

When I woke up, no cup of tea was steaming on my bedside table. Instead there was a note. I'd never seen Phoebe's handwriting. She'd had very good penmanship and a steady hand when she was young.

> *Dear Josh,*
> *I have written to your mother to say good-bye. I am sure she will understand that I am a girl in love. He is far above my station in life, and so I thought it hopeless. Perhaps that is how Aaron was able to bring me to your time. I had often thought of running away.*

Please thank him for offering to send me back with his time machine. But I do believe my time is drawing to an end anyway, and I may find my own way back. My brief absence may just make my beloved's heart grow fonder. I know now that nothing can keep us apart.

She didn't sign her name. She might have left before she had the . . . time.

The rest of the weekend was all downhill from there. Heather told me she was never speaking to me again because I'd ratted on her. In fact, she kept on telling me. Mom told Heather that her party dress was going back to Bloomingdale's, but she wasn't going anywhere. She was grounded until she was thirty. Heather told Mom it didn't matter because she was shamed for life. It was as simple as that. Camilla Van Allen would drop her like a hot potato. And we were all lost without Phoebe.

Then on Sunday night, Dad didn't call from Chicago. You wait and wait for weekends, but they're not always that great.

Aaron wasn't on the bus Monday morning, but I found him in the Black Hole before homeroom. I showed him Phoebe's note. After all, it was really for him too. I told him all about Phoebe, then and . . . now.

He was interested, but not that much. He was already word-processing something on one of the computers, and his mind was basically on that. He's always up to something.

"Josh, are you losing total track of time?" he said.

"Tomorrow's Parents' Night. We've got to get our act together about the history of Huckley School. Mr. Thaw will be all over us. He told us our entire grades were riding on this."

"They took Mr. Thaw off to Lenox Hill Hospital," I said. "Remember?"

"But he's back," Aaron said, not looking up from the screen. "He was the first teacher in school this morning. He probably thinks Cuthbert in the classroom was a figment of his imagination or whatever. He probably thinks he was some kid wandering in from public school to clean Buster's clock. Anyway, he's back."

"Is Buster back?"

"I don't know about Buster. He'll probably take the week off. After all, he got punched out with witnesses. What's that going to do for his self-esteem? If he's here, he'll be down with a counselor. Forget that. Concentrate on our report."

His screen was filling up with a report. But he hadn't printed out anything yet.

"So what have we got here?" he said. "Once upon a time there was a row of townhouses just off Central Park, with four families living in them."

"The Havemeyers, the Huckleys, the Van Allens, and the Vanderwhitneys," I said. "We don't know squat about the Havemeyers and the Huckleys."

"We'll get Mrs. Newbery on that," Aaron said. "What are media specialists for anyway? And in 1929 these four townhouses were recycled as Huckley School, right?"

"Works for me," I said.

The bell for homeroom rang. "I hate being interrupted by school," Aaron muttered. But then he came out of his chair. "Yessssss!" he said, doing his war dance.

"No, Aaron," I said. "Forget about it. We're not doing a demonstration of your cellular-reorganization formula for our history report. We're not doing our vanishing act with witnesses. And what if we got Cuthbert again?"

"You kidding?" he said. "That's top secret. That's not information you put into the hands of parents and teachers. But we already have somebody from the past—a living legend."

"Not Phoebe," I said. "Not Mrs. Van Allen. She's real old, and she treasures her privacy. It wouldn't be fair."

"Not Phoebe," Aaron said. "Mr. L. T. Thaw. He'll be at the meeting anyway, won't he? Parents' Night isn't required for parents, but it's required for teachers. Am I right? We'll just call on him."

"You call on him," I said. "I'm not calling on him."

"Boys," Mrs. Newbery said from the door, "it's time you cut along for Mr. Headbloom's homeroom. Why do I have to remind you of this every morning of my entire existence?"

Parents' Night was in the auditorium of Huckley House, and there was a good turnout. Aaron's parents were there somewhere in the throng. Mom and Heather came. Heather had plea-bargained to be let out of the apartment for school-related events. By the weekend she'd probably be a free woman. She'd already been on the phone with Camilla. I knew because it was my phone.

Aaron and I had to sit in the front row with the rest of the people taking bows, doing acts, and making reports. Mr. Thaw had made sure we were on the program, and in it:

Josh Lewis and Aaron Zimmer will present
a brief report on the colorful and aristocratic
origins of Huckley School, founded 1929.

The president of the parents' organization and the headmaster sat right behind us. Aaron and I were in freshly pressed dress code. We weren't the first item on the program. There were introductions and rounds of applause while the upper-school squash team, lacrosse team, and hockey team held up their trophies. An all-school string trio sawed out a couple of selections from *Beauty and the Beast*. A chorus of lower-school first graders in ball caps and long shirts did an original rap:

Huckley be the best
forget about the rest

The whole lower school seems to be turning into rappers.

"Kids," Aaron said.

We finally got around to middle-school reports. But then Aaron and I still had to sit through a long science-class demonstration with pig embryos. Fishface Pierrepont gave his lecture on

> Collecting classic comic books for
> fun and your investment portfolio

Then it was time for Aaron and me. It was getting late, and the audience was restless. We speeded up our presentation and charged through it.

"Picture it," Aaron began, looking around the too-tall podium at the audience. "Four high-profile New York families whose fortunes were amassed before confiscatory income tax. Picture them in the 1920's in four hard-to-heat white-elephant houses and about to make the move into the modern, climate-controlled grandeur of new Park Avenue buildings even then rising along their eastern flank."

"The Havemeyers," I said, taking over. Then I gave a rundown on this family from sources Mrs. Newbery looked up for us.

"The Huckleys," I said, "who gave their name and a bunch of money to our school." Then I went over them and moved on to the Van Allens. When we came to the Vanderwhitneys, I let Aaron take over.

"No name rings louder in the annals of American wealth and privilege," Aaron said in a ringing voice, "than the Vanderwhitneys."

He summed up a century or so of their family tree, working up to Mr. and Mrs. Osgood Vanderwhitney.

"Mrs. Vanderwhitney's second husband," Aaron explained, "was the once well-known man about town,

Mr. Thaw. We are honored to have on Huckley School's faculty a man who was born a Vanderwhitney and is the adopted son of Mrs. Vanderwhitney's second husband."

The audience of parents was getting a little confused by this, though there are plenty of second marriages among them too. And in the Zimmers' case, third.

"And so Josh and I introduce to you the last living link between Huckley School and the families who founded it, Mr. Lysander Theodore Thaw, our old—our history teacher. Step up and say a few words, Mr. Thaw." Aaron blinked out into the auditorium. Then he and I filed off the stage and went back to our seats.

From the back of the room came the sound of creaking joints. Then Mr. L. T. Thaw began to stalk down the aisle to a growing wave of polite applause. He limped to the podium.

From behind us, the president of the parents said to the headmaster, "The poor old duffer. We really must find a way to retire him."

Mr. Thaw frowned over the audience like they were history class. But this was his moment, maybe his last. Pulling on his beard, he launched into his boyhood in Vanderwhitney House. He dealt briefly with his mother running off with Mr. Thaw. He left out how his father had taken a dive onto Wall Street. But the more he talked, the more he remembered. He even recalled a pretty nursery maid from England who married the Van Allen boy from next door.

His old hands gripped the podium, and now he had

the audience listening and interested. After all, he's a living legend. Then he was winding down.

"And last but not least," he said, "I remember my dear brother Cuthbert, gone to his reward these many years, but as clear in my mind as if I'd seen him last week. Cuthbert is gone but not forgotten as the fire commissioner of the City of New York."

Mr. Thaw even took a bow. Then he tottered off the stage to more applause.

So that was Parents' Night. Our entire grade in History depended on it. But Aaron and I weren't worried.

"Now I can get back to my formula," he said on our way up the aisle. "We're talking new windows of opportun—" But then his voice broke. He went from high alto to baritone and back again. It was like cracking the sound barrier.

"Yikes," he said. "My voice is beginning to change. What's puberty going to do to my Emotional Component?"

A lot of the dads in the audience had gone to Huckley School. They made a ring around old Mr. Thaw because he'd been their teacher too. They must have forgotten how crusty he is because they were shaking his hand. They seemed to be thanking him. His old pink eyes were moist.

The crowd parted, and I was looking for Mom and Heather. But then I saw Dad. My dad.

He was there beside Mom, and they were kind of looking at each other. Heather was beside them. In fact, she was beside herself. "This is just like *Oprah*," she breathed, practically jumping up and down.

Dad spotted me. I wasn't sure what to do. I thought maybe we should shake hands. But he put out his arms and gave me a big hug. We gave each other a big hug.

"Have you grown?" He looked me over.

"Not an inch," I said.

"Plenty of time," Dad said.

"But how did you even know about Parents' Night?" I asked him. I hadn't told him about it. I didn't think he'd fly in from Chicago.

"I got a phone call late last Friday night. Must have been midnight your time. A young lady called me. She told me you had a report to give for Parents' Night. She told me it was my responsibility to be here. She was pretty definite about it. English too, I think."

Phoebe. I could picture her looking up Dad's number in Mom's address book. I could picture her young finger punching up Dad's area code.

Phoebe, one last time.

The four of us went home together. Mom and Dad, Heather and me. I don't know if Dad's home for good. We'll see. Plenty of time.

Richard Peck was born in Decatur, Illinois. He attended Exeter University in England and holds degrees from DePauw University and Southern Illinois University.

In 1990 he received the American Library Association's Margaret A. Edwards Award, which honors "an author whose book or books, over a period of time, have been accepted by young adults as an authentic voice that continues to illuminate their experiences and emotions, giving insight into their lives." His other books include *Are You in the House Alone?*, *Ghosts I Have Been*, *The Ghost Belonged to Me*, *Remembering the Good Times*, *Princess Ashley*, and, most recently, *The Great Interactive Dream Machine*.